KT-215-548

Get **more** out of libraries

Please return or renew this item by the last date shown.

You can renew online at www.hants.gov.uk/library

Or by phoning 0300 555 1387

Hampshire
County Council

man was

C016272531

Kate Walker was born in Nottingham, in the UK, but grew up in West Yorkshire. She met her husband at university in Wales and originally worked as a children's librarian. After the birth of her son she returned to her childhood love of writing. Her first book was published in 1984. She now lives in Lincolnshire with her husband—also a writer—and two cats who think they rule her life.

Books by Kate Walker

Mills & Boon Modern Romance

Destined for the Desert King
Olivero's Outrageous Proposal
A Question of Honour

Royal & Ruthless

A Throne for the Taking

Return of the Rebels

The Devil and Miss Jones

The Powerful and the Pure

The Return of the Stranger

Italian Temptation!

The Proud Wife

The Greek Tycoons

The Greek Tycoon's Unwilling Wife
The Good Greek Wife?

Visit the Author Profile page at
millsandboon.co.uk for more titles.

INDEBTED
TO MORENO

BY
KATE WALKER

First Published in Great Britain 2016
By Mills & Boon, an imprint of HarperCollins*Publishers*
1 London Bridge Street, London, SE1 9GF

© 2016 Kate Walker

ISBN: 978-0-263-91652-2

Our policy is to use papers that are natural, renewable and recyclable
products and made from wood grown in sustainable forests. The logging
and manufacturing processes conform to the legal environmental
regulations of the country of origin.

Printed and bound in Spain
by CPI, Barcelona

INDEBTED
TO MORENO

For Alison and Malcolm, aka Malison—a fine poet and my favourite Tech Support guy. With many happy memories of Writers' Holidays and other events.

PROLOGUE

THE ALMOST FULL moon was burning cold and high in the darkness of the sky as Rose slipped out of the door, shutting it cautiously behind her. She winced inwardly as the battered wood creaked on rusted hinges, the sound seeming appallingly loud in the stillness of the night, and froze in a panic, waiting for someone to stir upstairs, to come after her as her stepfather had done on that day almost three months ago. But the house remained silent and still, apparently empty, though she knew that there were half a dozen or so figures hidden behind the filthy, cracked windows on the upper floors.

She had to be grateful for the moonlight that illuminated her way down the weed-clogged path towards the street. It helped make sure that she didn't stumble over the beer cans or plastic bags of rubbish that littered her way. But for the few minutes it took her to reach the road and scurry out of sight, panic screamed a need to run along her nerves fighting a vicious battle with the need to move carefully and avoid making a sound. At any moment she expected to hear movement behind her, the sound of a shout waking and alerting everyone in the squat.

And one dangerous person in particular.

Rose's heart clenched as she tried to pull her thoughts away from the man she was leaving behind. A man she had once seen as her rescuer, coming to her aid when she needed help most. The man she now had to leave behind or lose herself once and for all.

It was a bitter irony that she had once seen this squat in the abandoned shell of a once elegant town house as a sanctuary as she'd fled the unwanted attentions of her hated stepfather, only to find that she had well and truly jumped from the frying pan into the fire.

'Oh, Jett…'

The name slipped past her lips, and, despite everything she did to push them away, images slid into her mind. The picture of his long, powerful body lying on the dusty floor of the bedroom they had claimed as their own, his head with the overlong jet-black mess of hair pillowed on the olive-skinned arms in which he hid his face. He had always slept like that, even after they had made burning, passionate love, tumbling deep into sleep as if at the press of a button. But she knew that the appearance of deep slumber was a false impression. One awkward move, the faintest sound and he would jolt awake in a moment, coming upright and alert in the space of a heartbeat, every wary sense on high alert.

He'd stirred in his sleep as she'd left his side and only by murmuring something about needing to use the toilet had she persuaded him to let his head drop back onto his arms.

'Don't be long' had been the curt, brief command and although she'd known he couldn't see her she had shaken her head, letting the long fall of her bright red hair conceal her face.

'I won't be a minute,' she'd managed, knowing that he wouldn't take that the way she meant it. She was not going to be absent from his side for just a minute but for ever. This would be her one and only chance to get out of here before all hell broke out and she was going to snatch at that chance and run with it.

Yet even as she ran down the road there was a terrible tearing sensation inside her, in the region of her heart. A sense of loss and yearning for what she had thought she had, for what she'd dreamed of, that now, with a bitter realisation, she knew to have been a fake all the time.

If only… But there was no room, no time for 'if only'. There was no future for her with this man, the man she had been foolish enough to fall head over heels for, to give herself body and soul to until she had realised the truth about the sort of person he was.

She should have known he was no knight on a white charger when he'd, literally, picked her up off the street. But then she'd been so lost and alone that she'd been grateful for any help, caught up in the dark spell he had woven around her from the start. Now she could no longer ignore the evidence that told her that Jett was involved in the abominable trade of dealing illegal drugs. A trade that had resulted in the horror of the death of one of the other squatters. She shuddered fearfully just thinking of it.

Which was why she had to get out of here right now. She had to go as far and as fast as she could and never once look back.

The sound of cars coming down the road caught her ears. She knew why they were there. The police had acted on her information, and their approach meant that time really had run out for her.

Speeding up, she dashed away from the house that had been the only thing she could call home for the last few months, breath catching in her lungs as, skidding slightly, she whirled around the corner. Behind her, the convoy of police cars came into the street and pulled up sharply outside the door to the squat.

It was over. But the real truth was that it had never truly begun and her naïve foolishness had blinded her to the reality until it was almost too late.

CHAPTER ONE

NAIRO ROJA MORENO stepped out of the door of his private jet and frowned savagely as the icy blast of air and rain crashed into his face, making him blink hard against the cold.

'Perdición!' he swore, pulling up the collar of his jacket, the wind whipping the word from his lips and whirling it up into the steel-grey sky. 'It's raining!'

Of course it was raining. This was England, and it seemed that the weather had conspired to remind him just how much he loathed the place.

London, where he'd once thought his life might start afresh only to find that what was left of his heart had been taken and carelessly discarded without a second thought.

'No.'

He made his way down the steps, tossing back his hair in defiance at the weather. The memories that swirled in his thoughts had nothing to do with the temperatures, except for the fact that it had always been cold in that damn house. Cold and miserable except for the times that he had been able to persuade Red to join him in the tatty, inadequate sleeping bag.

Be honest. It wasn't the weather or the house that had got to him. It was the coldness of betrayal. The coldness of a heart he had once thought was warm and giving. Until she had left him with nothing when she had vanished out of his life and into the night.

Well, good riddance to her, he told himself, shaking off his memories in the same moment as he slid into the car that was waiting for him. He had had no inclination to go after her, and there had been no time to even consider it. He had been so occupied turning his life around and making his way back to his family—a reconciliation that she had almost destroyed by her actions—that she had been the last thing on his mind. He'd managed a second chance and he wasn't going to stuff it up. This trip to London would be the final part of the task he had set himself.

'Dacre Street,' he told the driver in response to the man's request for a destination. He could only hope the driver knew where the damn place was; it was in no part of the London he usually frequented.

Nairo settled back on the seat, frowning darkly as he raked his wet hair back from his face. He had to get into the city, do the job he'd come to do, keep his promise to Esmeralda. He had so much to make up to his sister and this one last thing to make her happy was what mattered. After this, his duty was done.

If there ever was a day when it was the worst possible moment for Louise to need to go home sick, then it had to be today, Rose told herself, sighing as she pushed back a floating strand of bright auburn hair that had escaped from the neat braid for the nth time. Obviously her normally efficient and organised assistant had been feeling worse than she had let on the previous day, if the state of the reception area was anything to go by. Everything needed tidying, and the diary that detailed today's appointments had been splashed with coffee, blurring the details.

Not that Rose needed any reminders. The appointment

had been made a week ago, the first contact being with a heavily accented voice on the other end of the phone. Nairo Roja Moreno's PA as she declared herself to be.

'Nairo Roja Moreno...' Rose murmured to herself as she considered the blurred words in the diary. The eldest son of an aristocratic Spanish family, his PA had informed her. And he wanted to talk to her about a wedding dress?

She'd meant to look up this Spaniard on the Internet last night, but her mother had been so unwell that it had taken all of her time and attention to get them both through the evening.

When she'd got the confirmation email she'd been over-joyed. It had seemed like a rescue mission arriving just in time. Caring for her mother through her illness had drained her resources, taken all her energy, mental and physical. She'd had no new commissions in an age. The mess of her marriage that had never been and the scandal that had followed it had seen to that. She was behind with the rent on the boutique, had barely been able to meet the costs of her flat. But if this Nairo Moreno really did want her to design his sister's wedding dress together with the bridesmaids' outfits, the flower girls and pageboys of which there seemed to be dozens, well, it might just save her from going under. Save her reputation publicly, save her life financially and perhaps even save her mother's life in reality.

Joy had endured a long and difficult battle with the cancer that had assailed her. She was weak and drained by chemotherapy, the operation, and was only just start-ing to recover. Any new shock, any extra stress might be dangerous, and, after all the time it had taken to rebuild their relationship from a perilously rocky point ten years before, Rose hated to think that everything could be de-stroyed now.

Her aristocratic visitor would be here any moment. Tapping her pen in a restless tattoo on the appointment book, Rose frowned as she looked out at the lashing rain that was splattering the plate-glass window of her design rooms. Not the best day to imagine a summer wedding.

Jett had hated the rain, particularly in the unheated squat. As a result, so many rainy days had been spent cuddled up together...

A rush of dark memories swamped her mind, loosening her grip so that the pen dropped from her hand, falling to the floor and rolling away under a display cabinet.

'Darn it!'

Getting down on her hands and knees, she groped in the darkness, fumbling for the pen just out of reach. It was then that she heard the door open behind her, the rush of cold damp air telling her that someone had come into the building from the street.

'Sorry! Just a moment.'

'De nada.'

It was the sexiest voice, deep and dark and so beautifully accented.

Of course! The Spanish aristocrat—what was his name? Nairo something. Suddenly becoming aware of the way she must look, bottom in the air, narrow skirt stretched tight, she made one final lurch, banging her head on the shelf before grabbing the pen, then turning to push herself upwards.

It *was* no problem to wait, Nairo reflected. He was perfectly happy to stay here and enjoy the spectacle of a deliciously rounded bottom stuck up in the air as its owner groped for something under the shelving. Folding his arms across his chest, he leaned back against the door feeling his pulse kick up and thud hard and heavy in his veins as he enjoyed the view before him.

If there was one thing he hadn't anticipated on this unwanted trip to England, then it was the possibility of indulging in a little sensual pleasure. There was so much to be planned and organised back in Spain, with the demands of his sister's soon-to-be in-laws to take into consideration, that he had allowed himself only the freedom of a couple of days away from the chaos and uproar that The Wedding of the Century had created.

Now, with this tantalising display of female charms on display before him, he allowed himself to reconsider.

It had been a long time—too long—since he had had the pleasures of a woman in his bed. His father's final illness, the need for ferocious commitment to work on the family estates, restoring the Moreno fallen fortunes, and now, of course, Esmeralda's engagement and upcoming wedding had ensured that he had had little time to breathe.

Suddenly the prospect of a few days' relaxation, even in the grey, rainy city of London, had infinitely more appeal.

'Got it!'

The triumph in the woman's voice made him smile, but it was a smile that leached from his lips as he saw her lift her head.

Red hair. His personal curse. A bronze, auburn red it was true, not the bright red that had been one of the glories that he had so loved in the woman who had once filled his days, haunted his dreams.

Red...

The echo of his own voice sounded inside his head as memories threatened to surface. He had fought against those memories, pushing them behind him as he set about restoring his life to some degree of order and rebuilding it from the mess it had become. The last thing he wanted was the resurfacing of anything that connected him to the time when he had lived in London in such very different circumstances.

Scarlett. It was the name of this shop—the designer that Esmeralda had sent him to find—that had put these thoughts in his mind.

'I'm sorry— I— Ouch!' The sharp cry of pain broke into his thoughts.

She had lifted her head rather too quickly in her triumph at having found whatever it was she was looking for and so had caught her face on the side of the shelf. Immediately he moved forward, holding out his hand to her.

'Allow me...'

That voice was designed to turn any woman to mush, Rose told herself. And the firm, warm grip of his hand was like touching a live wire, sizzling reaction sparking all along her arm.

'Th-thank you.'

The sharp bang on her forehead had brought tears to her eyes so that she was blinking hard to clear them as he swung her to her feet, the strength of the movement bringing her up and close to him. So close that she almost fell against him as she rocked on her toes before she managed to snatch back her balance and settle her feet on the floor.

She was assailed by a rush of heat from the closeness of a powerful male body, her senses tantalised by the heady combination of the musky scent of clean male skin, a sensual tang of some citrusy aftershave, all topped off with the fresh, wild trace of rain and wind that he had brought in from the street outside.

Suddenly, shockingly, all she could think of was one word, one man, one memory.

Jett... The word slammed into her mind without thought, without control.

No!

Why was she thinking of him? It was almost ten years since the night she had fled from the squat. A decade in which she had picked herself up, dusted herself off and built her life back up again. To the stage where this Spanish aristocrat was here today to discuss a commission to design a wedding dress for his sister.

A commission that she desperately needed. It would be the first time ever she had been asked to design a dress outside the small spread of the local area, unless you counted the dress that her friend Marina Marriot had worn just last month at her wedding to an up-and-coming actor.

'I'm fine now...'

She wished she didn't sound quite so breathless. Wished she had let go of his hand before this so that it didn't look quite so embarrassing as she had to ease her fingers from his.

'De nada.'

Again the sound of that sexy accent coiled around her, bringing memories of another man who had spoken with just that hint of an exotic pronunciation.

But there was no way that Jett would wear a suit like this one that made this man look so sleek and powerful and magnificent. That had to have been custom-made to flatter the powerful straight shoulders, the width of his chest and the lean length of his legs down to where his feet in polished handmade shoes were firmly planted on the tiled floor. Jett had never owned a suit. Like her, he had barely had a change of clothes. The tee shirt and jeans she wore as she fled from the house where the unwanted attentions of her stepfather had made sure it had never felt like a home being the only items that she'd had to drape over the door to what was laughingly called their bedroom.

Her eyes had cleared now and she was looking up into the carved, hard features of the most stunning man she had ever seen. Amber eyes framed with impossibly lush, black lashes burned down into hers. Hard bones shaped the lean cheeks, touched with a darkness of stubble even this early in the day. That mouth was an invitation to sin, warm, sensual, full lips slightly parted over sharp white teeth.

And she knew how that mouth felt, how it tasted…

She felt the world tilt on its axis, the room swinging round her.

'Jett…'

There was no holding it back this time. She didn't even try. It escaped on a breath that was all she could manage as she realised just who this man was.

A man who had once filled her days and haunted her nights. Even when she had run from him she had still taken him with her in her thoughts, her nights filled with memories that jolted her awake, left her drenched in sweat, her heart pounding. A man she had had to hand over to the police when she had learned the source of the money he had suddenly come into, then left to face the repercussions of his actions.

'Jett?' She heard him echo her response sharply, a frown snapping the black, straight brows together, cold eyes looking down into her upturned face.

Those amazing eyes narrowed, the beautiful mouth tightening as his head came up and he took a step back, away from her.

'Red… I didn't know *you* worked here.'

Worked here. Perhaps that was a score one to the fact that he really was here by accident. That he hadn't sought her out—because why would he do that after all this time? The thought didn't help with the thumping of her heart, the feeling like the beating of a thousand butterfly wings in the pit of her stomach. He hadn't come looking for her and it was all just a terrible misstep of fate.

But that dark emphasis on the word *you* twisted something in her guts, bringing home an awareness of the fact that she was all alone, not even Louise in the office, within call. Tension stiffened her back, tightened her shoulders.

'And I didn't know *you* worked for Nairo Moreno.'

That brought an unexpected twist to his mouth, the sensual lips twitching into something that could have been described as a smile but was totally without any warmth in it. His eyes seemed to impale her where she stood.

'Not worked…I *am* Nairo Moreno. I came here to see Ms Cavalliero. Oh—what, my darling Red…?'

The smile grew wider, darker.

'Did you think I was here to see you? That I would have hunted you down after all this time, determined to find you?'

She had actually considered that fact, Nairo told himself. It was written all over her beautiful face. The young girl he had once known as 'Red' had always held the promise of being a looker, but he had never anticipated her growing into the sleek, sexy vision who stood before him.

That pert bottom that had caught his attention from the start was only a small part of a slim, shapely figure displayed to full advantage in the cream lace blouse and navy blue, clinging skirt. The hair that had once been the vivid, vibrant colour that gave her her nickname was now a more subtle auburn shade, still with the glint of red blending in with the glossy darker tones. Those almond-shaped, slightly slanting hazel eyes were even more feline than before when accentuated with the subtle use of cosmetics that she would never have been able to afford back then.

A swift, sharp inward shake of his head broke the train of his thoughts, dragging them back from the path down which they had wandered.

She was the last thing he wanted in his world right now.

Hadn't she come close to ruining his life all those years before? Ten years younger, and a lifetime more naïve, he had risked losing everything for the sake of a few short nights of heedless passion. He had even, foolishly, blindly, come close to giving her a piece of his heart. Only to discover that he had been nothing to her when the promise of a reward for information had more appeal instead.

'It's taken me rather a long time—don't you think? Ten years. So why should I suddenly turn round and want to see you again? You can relax about that, *Red*—I am not looking for you but for your boss.'

'My boss?'

'*Sí*. Ms Rose Cavalliero. The owner of this business, and the designer of...'

An autocratic wave of his hand indicated the two beautiful dresses displayed on mannequins in the corner of the room. Of course, Rose realised, he was here to discuss the design of his sister's wedding dress. But the realisation that he still thought she was only the receptionist, that he hadn't put two and two together to recognise that the 'Scarlett' in her business name was in fact her, was in no way eased by the thought of that commission he'd come to discuss.

Oh, no, no! She couldn't work for him. She wouldn't do it. OK, so it might mean a real coup for her business. A boost to her reputation that would be of immeasurable value. But would it be worth it?

All the money in the world couldn't compensate for spending time with Jett—with this Nairó Moreno as he now called himself. Even if he hadn't come looking for revenge, it was obvious that he could barely bring himself to be polite to her.

But how could she get out of it?

'So where is she?'

The question came coldly, curtly, and seeing the hard set of his face Rose was swamped by a rush of cold unease.

To see the smoulder of dark anger in his eyes made her feet feel unsafe on the floor, her mouth drying sharply. If only she had known who this Nairo Moreno really was, then she would never have agreed to meet him today.

But of course he didn't realise exactly who she was. He still believed that she was only the receptionist. For a second the desire to put him in his place by pointing out that she owned the whole establishment and was the designer he had said he so wanted to meet warred with a sense of self-preservation. What she really wanted was to get rid of him before he brought his malign influence back into her present as he had done to her past.

'She couldn't be here. Her mother isn't well.'

Well, that was true enough. And the closer she could get to the truth with this man, the less likely she was to give herself away.

'She didn't think to send a message to let me know?' The anger was there now, in a frigid form. 'That's hardly good business practice.'

'It—it was an emergency. She got called away unexpectedly.'

'I see.'

His tone said the exact opposite as he pushed back the immaculate white cuff of his shirt and checked the time. On the sort of platinum watch that the man she had once known could never have afforded.

Unless of course… The coldness at her spine turned into a slow, icy creeping sensation that made her remember just why she had had to run out on him, the darkness of the world that she had discovered she had fallen into.

'I'm sure she'll be in touch…'

When she had some excuse ready. Some reason why

she couldn't take on his commission. She'd think of something when she wasn't faced with telling it to him in person. Right now, all she wanted was for him to get out of her life and stay out. For good this time.

'I'll be waiting for her message.'

The dark thread of anger that laced the statement turned it into an unspoken threat, making her heart clench painfully so that she had to struggle to draw her next breath.

'I'll tell her.' Embarrassingly it was a revealing squeak.

Unable to meet those coldly assessing eyes, Rose hurried to the door, deliberately moving so as not to risk touching him, or come within reach of one of those long-fingered hands that now rested lightly on the smooth leather belt that encircled his narrow waist. She didn't want to remember anything about the touch of those hands, and the thought of them coming anywhere near her again set the butterflies fluttering wildly in her stomach all over again.

'You do that.'

This was not at all how he had expected the day to go, Nairo reflected as he watched this new Red march to the door and yank it open, standing there stiff and taut, rejection in every inch of her slender body. The meeting with some society designer he had anticipated had not happened and instead he had found himself confronted by memories from his past stirring the silt in which he'd believed they were buried.

Forcing him to remember how this one slip of a girl had turned his life upside down, blackening his name just when he was fighting to win back his father's respect, and then walked out on him.

To remember how soft her skin had felt, the warmth of her body as she had curled up to him on the rough and ready 'bed' that had been all the furniture their room had possessed. He could still catch her unique, individual scent even if now it was hidden under some crisp fresh perfume and it awoke a hunger he had thought he'd forgotten. A hunger that he had spent the last ten years trying to obliterate. He'd indulged his masculine needs indiscriminately but never, it seemed, managed to wipe it out. Not if it could be woken again so fast and so easily.

'As soon as I see her,' Red came back at him with what was clearly a pointed reminder that she wanted him to leave. And it was because she so obviously wanted him gone that, perversely, he found himself lingering.

She felt it too, this disturbing hot flood of memories and awareness. It was there in her face, in the wide darkness of her eyes, the pupils distended until they almost obliterated the mossy softness of her irises. Her breathing was tight and unnatural and he could see the faint blue tinge under the pale skin at the base of her neck where a pulse beat, rapid and uneven. A kick of reaction hit him in the gut, keeping him where he was instead of leaving as she clearly intended he should.

'Is she always this unprofessional?' he asked icily, watching as her mouth quivered, then tightened again.

How was it possible that after all this time he could remember how that soft mouth had tasted, the warm yielding of those pink lips against his own?

'She…has so many demands on her time. More than she can cope with sometimes.'

'She's so busy she can risk losing an important commission?'

Rose flinched inside at the sharp stab of the challenge. Just moments ago she had thought of the Moreno commission as the chance of a lifetime, a rescue package that had landed on her desk wrapped in beautiful paper and tied with golden ribbon. But now it was as if she had opened that magical parcel only to find it filled with black, stinking ashes, with a deadly poisonous snake lurking at the bottom just waiting to strike.

She had to get out of this contract somehow, but for now she would settle for having Jett—or Nairo as it seemed she must call him—out of the shop, out of her space, to give her time to think about the way she could possibly deal with this without ruining her professional reputation once and for all.

'I can't tell you about that.' The fact that it was actually the most honest thing she had said gave a new strength to her voice. 'So, if you don't mind…I'd like you to leave now.'

His smile was dark, devilish enough to send shivers down her spine.

'But we've only just found each other again.' The mockery that lifted his tone had the sting of poison.

'Well, you obviously haven't missed me in the past ten years.'

No, that sounded too much as if she regretted it. The last thing she wanted was for him to think that *she* had missed *him*, even if it was true. But all her courage had seeped away, leaving her feeling weak and empty, genuinely afraid of what she might spark off if she challenged him too strongly.

'I wish I could say it's been a pleasure to see you again, but I'm afraid that just wouldn't be true. And I really must ask you to leave now. We have this event—a bridal fashion show—tonight. I have to get ready for that.'

That she wanted him to go wriggled under his skin and stayed there, irritating him furiously. She'd got under his skin in a very different way in the past. He had let her do things to his heart that he had never allowed any other woman—any other human being except perhaps Esmeralda—to do to him before or since. But now that they had met up again, all that she wanted was to be rid of him as soon as possible.

The temptation to dig his heels in and refuse to move at all almost overwhelmed him. But a moment's thought left him realising that he didn't have to tackle this right now. Not yet. He knew where Red was; she wasn't going anywhere. He could afford the time to wait and discover rather more about her, and then he would act in the way that would give him the best satisfaction possible.

Shaking her life right to the roots just as she had done to his when she'd walked out on him, leaving behind a mess it had taken years to sort out.

A curt nod was his only response to her pointed remark. It amused him to see the way her shoulders dropped slightly in relief, the easing of the tension about her mouth as she believed that she had got rid of him.

'You'll tell Ms Cavalliero that *I* kept our appointment? And I expect to meet up with her at her earliest convenience.'

Left to himself he'd dispense with the designer and her frills and fancies and go straight to the result he most wanted—the settling of the score he had with the woman he'd only ever known as Red. But he'd promised Esmeralda and he wasn't prepared to take any risks with his sister's health that not keeping that promise might result in.

So he'd see to this damn dress—the dress of his sister's dreams—first. And then he'd deal with Red. He'd waited nearly ten long years already. He reckoned he could wait a little while longer.

The burn of his memories suddenly flamed up again, hot and hard, as he saw the way that she stood at the door, stiff-shouldered, taut-backed, her chin lifted in a sign of defiance. There was a flare of awareness in those mossy-golden eyes that pushed him just too close to the edge of the restraint he was holding so tight.

His feet came to a sudden halt, not letting him move forward. He caught her swiftly indrawn breath, noted the extra tension in every muscle that held her slim frame tight, drew in her stomach and lifted the swell of her pert breasts above the embroidered belt that circled her waist.

'Red...'

If only he knew how much she hated that once affectionate nickname! That focussed stare held her transfixed, unable to look away in spite of the fact that she felt as if his gaze were searing through her skin, burning her eyes to dust. Slowly he lifted a hand, touched her face, the blunt tips of his long fingers resting so lightly on the cheekbone under her right eye.

'I never thought I'd see you again,' he said flatly. 'It's been...interesting...meeting up like this.'

'*Interesting*—that isn't the word I'd use to describe it.'

Devastating, earth-shaking, came closer. So many times in the past she'd dreamed of just this meeting happening— and dreaded it in the same moment.

'But I need to tell you. I am not the man that I was.'

'I can see that. That is, if Moreno is really your name,' she challenged.

'Jett was only ever a nickname. Moreno is my family name, though I didn't use it then—before.'

Abruptly his mood changed, his eyes becoming darker.

'They let me go, you know,' he said. 'There was no evidence against me.'

The conversational tone of his voice was at odds with what she read in the taut muscles of his face. Just how had Jett become this Nairo Moreno?

The man who stood before her was light years away from the wild, rough-haired youth she had once known.

The one who had stolen her heart only to break it just a few weeks later, crushing it brutally under his booted foot. Was he the member of a Spanish aristocratic family he claimed to be or—that nasty slimy feeling slithered down her spine again, making her shiver—had his obvious wealth and position been bought with the proceeds of other activities in the years since they had known each other? There might have been no evidence of the crime she'd suspected him of, but he had clearly come a long way in ten years and that spoke of a ruthlessness and focus that few men possessed.

Something she didn't want to dig into too deeply. And a very good reason to get out of the contract to design a dress for anyone in his family if she possibly could.

'You will not tell anyone about the time we knew each other.'

It was a cold-blooded command, laced through with a powerful seam of threat, a warning as to what would happen if she was fool enough to reveal anything he wanted kept hidden.

'Not even Ms Cavalliero.'

'I doubt if she'd need to know.' Not when she already knew every dark detail about Nairo Roja Moreno. And wished she didn't. 'I certainly won't be telling.'

'Make sure you don't.'

The finger that rested on her cheek traced a slow, gentle path down the line of her jaw, to rest against the corner of her mouth, hooded eyes watching every flicker of expression across her face.

It was all that Rose could do not to turn her head sharply, pull away from that small, lingering touch. She wanted to move, desperately longed to back away, and yet at the same time that simple touch was so familiar, bringing back memories of the feel of his hands on her skin, the taste of his mouth…

She couldn't go there. She *mustn't* go there!

'Take your hand off my face.' She hissed the words out as much against the feelings that were stinging her as at him. 'I didn't give you permission to touch me and I...'

She couldn't continue in the face of his unexpected soft laugh and the way that he deliberately twisted his hand so that the backs of his fingers were now against her skin. Deliberately he stroked his fingers down her cheek again.

'I said don't do that!' This time she couldn't hold back and jerked her head away in angry rejection.

His laughter scoured her spine, but he lifted his hand slowly, bronze eyes gleaming with wicked mockery.

'My, you do have a tendency to overreact, *querida*. It didn't use to be that way. I can recall a time when you would beg for my touch.'

'Then you must have an amazing memory. It was a very long time ago.'

'Not long enough,' Nairo drawled, the smile evaporating fast. 'Some things you just don't forget.'

'Really? Well, I'm afraid my recollection isn't as good as yours—and it's certainly not something I want to revive.'

Making the movement look as if she were only wanting to ease his departure, she slipped away from him, holding open the door again.

'I'll pass on your messages.'

The words showed every trace of the effort she was making to get them out, fighting against giving in to the burning response even that most gentle of touches was sparking off all over her skin. One flick of a glance up at him was more than she could cope with. She could see herself reflected in those burnished eyes, small and diminished in a way that made her legs feel weak as cotton wool.

'I'll tell her—everything you said.'

'Except that you knew me before.'

How did he manage to inject such deadly poison into six simple words? The stepfather she had run from in a flight that had ended up with her living in the squat might have ranted and roared, bellowing threats, but he had never managed to make her quail inside in the way that this quietly spoken command could do.

'Except for that,' she managed jerkily.

For another dangerous moment his fingers still lingered too close to her face, but then, just as she thought that she couldn't keep control any longer, he lifted his hand away and let it drop to his side. The smile that he flashed on and off was like burning ice, no emotion at all in it.

'See you around, Red.'

'Not if I see you first.'

The words were muttered to an empty space. He'd gone, striding out into the darkness and the rain without a single glance back. It was as if defiance of his presence was all that had been holding her upright as she sagged back against the wall and let the door slam back into place.

He was gone. And she was free, safe—for now.

But it was only a temporary reprieve. There was no way she could hold off having Jett—in the form of Nairo Moreno—back in her life while he still wanted to see Rose Cavalliero. Right now he had no idea that *she was* the Rose he'd come to talk to, but she couldn't hope to let that last for very much longer. He would put two and two together, and when he did, then he would be back.

She had to get rid of him; she couldn't cope with him intruding into her life. Not just because of the past but because of the shocking effect he still had on her today.

Slowly her hand crept up to her face, covering the spot where Nairo's fingertip had touched her. She almost expected it to have etched a brand into her skin, marking

her as his. He had done that long ago, hadn't he? He had
touched her life and encircled her with bands of emotional
and sexual steel so that she had never been able to break
free. Even now, all these years later, he could still invade
her life and if she wasn't careful he would leave it in ruins
all over again.

CHAPTER TWO

He should never have let himself touch her.

Nairo slid his car into the nearest empty parking space, stamped on the brakes with uncharacteristic lack of care and switched off the engine. His concentration had been shot all afternoon, in a way so untypical of him that it felt as if he was teetering on the edge of a form of madness. The tips of his fingers still seemed to burn with the imprint of that touch, the connection of skin on skin, even though it was hours since he had walked out of the shop and left Red behind. He was sure that if he brought his hand close to his face he would still inhale the perfume of her skin, the fresh, unique combination that was this woman mixed with the light floral scent she had worn.

Or perhaps that was because the cloud of her personal body perfume seemed to enclose him ever since he had realised just who she was. It had been like that after they had first become lovers. In the squat she had always washed every day, even in the freezing water that was all they had available, and the scent of her skin had been the only thing that was fresh or clean in the grubby little room that they had called 'home'.

Waking up each morning to find her curled against him, the soft hair, longer and redder than she wore it now, falling over her face, had made him feel as if life was worth living at a time when he had had serious doubts on that matter.

She'd had her own problems too. Running from an aggressive and abusive stepfather, a mother who had been too weak to protect her, she had still given him a reason to wake up—if only because waking up usually meant another opportunity to take her in his arms, and give in to the heated passion that burned into his soul every time he touched her.

He had even thought about changing his life for her.

'Change—for her—hah!'

The words punched into the air as he pushed open the door to the hall where the wedding fayre was being held, the violence of the movement expressing the way the memories burned like acid.

He had thought about change—had even taken the first steps towards it—and she...she had just walked out on him, never looking back. She'd also added an extra little sting to her departure that had come close to ruining every chance he had had of rebuilding what was left of his relationship with his family.

The burn of that memory almost had him turning and marching right back out again. He wanted nothing to do with Red—and yet he couldn't get her out of his mind. Her betrayal, her desertion, demanded some sort of retribution and yet he had no wish to tangle himself up with her all over again. He had just about found peace after ten years' hard work. Did he really want to stick his head right back in the lion's mouth and risk it all over again?

But the promise he had made to Esmeralda held him prisoner. He had sworn he would bring her this designer she had set her heart on, and he was not going back on his word. Only with that contract secured and his sister happy would he consider just how he would deal with Red.

The sound of the buzz of many voices from the end of the corridor told him just where the event was being held and had him heading towards the glass-paned door.

The noise of conversation hit him along with a strong wave of perfume—a heady mixture of so many different fragrances. The room was full of women of all ages, shapes and sizes. There were flowers everywhere too, and a small runway set up in the centre of the hall with a white floor, leading to a fall of heavy velvet curtains in rich red. The colours of the flowers, the curtains, the women's dresses and suits whirled and blurred into a kaleidoscopic haze.

'And now, ladies, we have a special treat for you…'

The voice was immediately familiar and Nairo cursed under his breath. Because there she was again. The woman he had known as Red.

If he had felt that she had grown into a beautiful woman when he had first seen her in the boutique, then this was even worse. Now she was groomed, and sleek, elegant in a silky peacock-blue shift dress, simple and sleeveless, that clung lovingly all the way from the softly scooped neck, over the curves of breasts and hips to end just above her knees and reveal a heart-jolting slender length of leg. The ridiculously high-heeled shoes were exactly the same colour as the dress, except for a perky little white bow at the toe. The whole effect had him clenching his hands into tight fists and pushing them deep into the pockets of his trousers as he fought with his immediate and primitive response.

He'd thought he'd put her out of his mind. He'd tried his damnedest to do just that, but it had taken only one look, one touch, and it had become obvious just why he'd been hooked in that way. She'd had the power to entrance him as a skinny girl and now she'd grown up, matured, he was swamped by a hunger he hadn't felt before or since. Then he'd been naïve enough to label it with a softer emotion because then he'd been fool enough to believe that emotion existed. He'd soon learned his lesson.

Now was not the time he wanted to remember how he had once been able to hold one slender foot in his hand, lift it to his mouth and kiss it from the long, delicate toes all the way up to where her legs disappeared under her skirt…

…and beyond.

Infierno! He could feel an unwanted heat flooding his body, hardening him and making his heart pulse in a hungry response to the erotic memory that had him in its grip. Violently he shook his head to drive it away and only succeeded in drawing the attention of the women closest to him. Their expressions of surprise and the widening of their eyes a sure giveaway of how unexpected his presence was, here in this ultra-feminine environment.

Nairo ruthlessly determined to ignore them—he had no interest in any woman here except for Red—and the important designer, wherever she was. He pointedly directed his gaze towards the runway, and the woman on it, her auburn hair gleaming glossily under the spotlight.

He watched Red lift the microphone again and announce, 'As I said—a real treat—for the first time ever an exclusive preview of my brand-new designs for spring.' *My*.

The word exploded inside Nairo's head, battering at his thoughts. *My brand-new designs…*

Of course—he'd been a complete fool. How could he have not realised? It had all been there in front of him, but he had been so set on his mission for Esmeralda—and so stunned to find himself face-to-face with Red after all these years—that his intelligence had failed him and he hadn't made the connections that he should have done.

Red. *Scarlett*. The name written above the window of

the small boutique. And the designer's name was Rose Cavalliero.

Rose red. *Scarlett.*

The velvet curtains had opened and a model had emerged from behind them, walking up the runway, her progress marked by gasps of delight and admiration. She was a willow-slim beauty, and the dress she was wearing was a masterpiece of lace and silk, a fairy-tale wedding gown.

But he spared it only one brief glance. There was no space in his mind to focus on anything but the woman who stood on the side of the runway, microphone in hand, talking about trains, beading, boned bodices…

All he could think was that *she*—Red—was also Rose Cavalliero—

Scarlett's talented designer—the one his sister dreamed of having to create a dress for her upcoming wedding.

The woman he had once known as Red was the woman he had come to London to meet—and to persuade her to come back to Spain with him.

Suddenly the room that had already felt so alien to him in its total focus on femininity, the overwhelming reek of clashing perfumes, seemed to constrict around him, the lights dimming. It couldn't be any further from the rooms in his father's home where he had lived as a boy. The old-fashioned high-walled castle so wrongly named Castillo Corazón—the castle of the heart! But the feeling of being trapped was just the same.

As an adolescent, he had felt this sensation of being cornered when his new stepmother had insisted that he meet all her female friends—the wives or daughters of acquaintances, some of whom had once been or still were his father's mistresses. They had almost mobbed him, circling round him like brightly painted predators. He had learned fast and young to recognise when someone was genuine and when they were fake.

Or he'd thought he had.

He hadn't recognised the secrets behind Red's green eyes. And he had known the slash of betrayal when he had found out the truth.

'And perhaps for an older bride, this elegant look…'

The clear, confident voice carried perfectly, no real need for the microphone, but it was not the woman on the runway whom Nairo was seeing. Instead it was the woman he had met in the boutique that morning.

Hell, she'd still deceived him even then. She had known who he was, known that he had come to see *her*, and yet she had let him linger in his belief that she was just the receptionist and that Rose Cavalliero was someone else entirely.

She had had the opportunity to tell him the truth then, but she hadn't taken it. Instead she had dodged the issue, kept it to herself, and then she'd dismissed him once again in a brief and curt email.

Scowling, Nairo remembered the message that had reached him in his suite just an hour and a half ago. Rose Cavalliero was sorry, but she was afraid that she couldn't manage to fit in a meeting with him after all. She apologised for the inconvenience, but the truth was that she wasn't taking on any more commissions at the moment. She was sorry that he had been inconvenienced in coming to London for nothing, but she needed to take time to care for her mother…

Coldly polite but dismissive. All of which could only mean that she had something to hide.

'And this is the highlight of the Spring Collection. I've named it the Princess Bride.'

Perhaps it was the name, perhaps it was the sound of the

murmurs of appreciation that flowed around the room, but something made Nairo look up to see yet another model emerging from behind the scarlet curtains.

In that instant he knew just why Esmeralda had been so insistent that this particular designer should create her dress. If she could make these women—every one of them—look so stunning, then what would she do for his sister? She would turn his shy, uncertain sibling into a glorious beauty—the princess she was meant to be—and surely that would give Esmeralda the confidence to face up to Duke Oscar's critical and demanding family without making herself ill again. And that was what he owed to his sister.

A memory stirred in his mind. The image of Esmeralda when he had come back from Argentina, where his father had sent him as penance for his adolescent rebellion. His sister had always been slim, but then she had been frail and delicate as a tiny bird. He'd even been afraid to hug her in case she might break. It had torn at his conscience to realise that the truth was that she was suffering from anorexia. It had taken him months to encourage her to let go her hold on her appetite and eat.

There and then he'd vowed that he would never let her down again. That he would do whatever it took to make her happy—keep her healthy and strong. To do that he now had to bring Rose Cavalliero back with him. Even if she had turned out to be the woman he had known all those years ago.

And when he had Red—or Rose or whatever her name was—in the castle in Andalusia, then he could tie up all the loose ends that were left hanging from when they had been together before. He would get rid of this unwelcome desire that still made him burn for her and he would teach her how it had felt to be the one cast aside when something better presented itself.

Leaning back against the wall, he folded his arms and prepared to wait and watch until it was time to talk to her.

Rose had been so focussed on the fashion show and making sure that everything ran smoothly that she had had no time at any point to actually look up and take notice of the crowd. But now, with the last dress displayed and the final parade of models down the runway, she could relax and look up, take a breath, glance out across the room…

And that was when she saw him.

Apart from the fact that Nairo Moreno was the only male in the room, it was impossible to miss him. He was leaning against the wall, arms folded, dressed all in black, with his shirt open loose at the neck. Like a big dark bird of prey amongst a flock of gaudy, chattering parrots. The burn of his golden-eyed stare was like a laser beam coming across the room.

He must have read the email she'd sent trying to get out of the commission he wanted. She'd asked for a receipt, so she knew he'd opened it. But he had determined to ignore it. She'd tried to avoid telling him who she was—who the designer Rose Cavalliero really was—but it seemed she'd failed miserably. Because now he was here—waiting, watching like some dark sentinel at the door.

'Rose!'

'Ms Cavalliero!'

Belatedly becoming aware of the way that she had been standing, silent and stunned, while her audience grew restless, Rose blinked hard, clearing her eyes of the haze of panic that had blurred her vision and forced herself to focus. At the front of the audience were the special guests, the reporters who had been invited specially in the hope of giving the new collection a great opening. That even more hopefully would lead to the sort of sales that would save her business, pay the rent for another twelve months. Give her mother a place to live and rest as she recovered from the draining bouts of chemotherapy. They'd only just found each other again properly; she couldn't bear it if their time together was so short.

Dragging her gaze away from the dark figure at the door, she switched on what she hoped was a convincing smile as she turned her attention to the first reporter to get to her feet—a well-known fashion writer for a luxury magazine.

'Do you have a question?' she managed. 'I'm happy to answer...'

'I'm glad to hear that.'

It wasn't the fashion reporter who spoke but another woman, a blonde she hadn't spotted before. Rose's heart sank. She knew this woman and so what was coming.

'Don't you think it's something of an irony, the fact that you are publicising your new collection now—with images of love and happy-ever-afters—when your own story is so very different?'

The bite in her voice was unmistakeable, sharp as acid. Rose recognised her as Geraldine Somerset, a person she had seen at one of Andrew's parties. The woman everyone had expected to be his fiancée before he'd met Rose.

'I don't know what you mean.'

'Oh, I'm sure you do.'

Geraldine lifted a newspaper that had been lying on her chair. Rose had no need to see it to know that it was a notorious scandal rag. She also knew just what headline the woman wanted everyone to see. Geraldine unfolded the sheet to its full length, waved it above her head, turning so that everyone could read the banner headline: *'Dream-maker or dream-breaker?'*

Rose even knew what pictures went with that story. How could she not when a copy of just that paper had been pushed through her letter box less than a week ago? On one side of the text was a picture of Andrew, head down, frowning and glum. The other was a picture of Rose herself, striding into her boutique—the name Scarlett perfectly clear and in focus. It had been taken shortly after the news of the broken engagement, the cancelled wedding, had hit the fan.

'Would you want to buy your wedding dress from a woman who only cancelled her own marriage just three days before the ceremony?' Geraldine was demanding now. 'Would you entrust the most important day of your life—or your daughter's—to someone who had so little care about her fiancé that she left him broken-hearted practically at the altar?'

'That isn't the way it was...' Rose protested, only to have the newspaper waved even more violently in rejection of her words.

"Dream-maker or dream-breaker?"' Geraldine declared, clearly very proud of the headline it was obvious she had created.

It was equally apparent that she was having the effect she wanted. The whole mood of the evening had changed. The murmurs of appreciation and approval that had marked the end of the fashion show had now changed to darker, more critical comments. Already people were pushing back their chairs, getting to their feet.

'This has nothing to do with my work!' Rose tried, but it was like Canute asking the sea to go back. Everything had changed and Geraldine, with her emotive headline, the carefully slanted photographs, had turned the tide of opinion.

Rose had forgotten that Nairo Moreno was here. That he was watching all this.

The moment the thought had crossed her mind she lost her concentration as she flicked a hasty, nervous glance to where Nairo leaned against the wall by the door. Or rather, where Nairo had been leaning. Even as she watched she saw his eyes narrow sharply, the beautiful, sensual mouth tighten until it was just a thin, hard line. The frown that snapped his black brows frankly terrified her.

Not meeting her eyes, his gaze fixed on the scene before him, he levered himself up from his position and stood tall and dark and powerful as he surveyed the room.

'The woman's bad luck—she taints everything she touches.' Geraldine was getting into full flow again, her voice rising to almost a screech, the newspaper flapping wildly as she waved it high. 'I mean—who would want *her* to design a dress…?'

'I would.'

Cold and clear, the response cut through the buzz of outrage and comment that had filled the room. The silence that fell was as if a huge blanket had been dropped over everyone, stifling any sound. The audience stilled too, as Nairo moved forward, his movements the dangerous prowl of a predatory wild cat. A path opened up to let him through and even Geraldine froze to the spot, her words deserting her as he came closer.

Rose couldn't blame her. Seen like this, Nairo Moreno was the sort of man who could suck all the air out of a room simply by existing. She found herself struggling to breathe, waiting and watching…

'I said *I would*.'

Nairo had reached Geraldine's side now and he snatched the newspaper away from her, sparing it only the briefest, iciest glance before he crushed it brutally in one hand

and tossed it aside, contempt in every inch of his powerful body.

'I would have Miss Cavalliero design a dress for someone I loved. Anyone with eyes to see would do the same—
wouldn't you?' he challenged, his fierce gaze raking over
the rest of the audience. 'Anyone but a fool could see that
as a designer Miss Cavalliero is hugely skilled. As a man,
I'm no expert in fashion...'

Rose watched in amazement as he actually shrugged
his shoulders in a gesture of assumed self-deprecation.

It had to be assumed, didn't it? Even as the Jett she'd
known he wouldn't willingly admit to any sort of weakness in his own make-up. But the gesture had worked.
The women surrounding him had actually smiled. Some
of them were nodding.

'But even I can see that these dresses are works of art.'

He had the room in the palm of his hand, Rose realised.
He was turning the tide of disapproval that Geraldine had
threatened to direct against her.

'Miss Cavalliero...'

Nairo had moved closer, was holding out a hand to her.
For the space of a dazed heartbeat she stared at it, only
realising after a moment that he meant to help her down
from the runway, onto the floor of the main ballroom.

She needed that help. Needed the support of his strength
and the warm power of that hand. But even as his grip
closed over her fingers, she knew a sudden stunning
change, felt the sting of burning electricity fizz through
her so that the hold she took on him was more than to get
down the steps to the floor. It was like being taken back in
years, to the days when she had been just a stupid, crazy,
hormone-ridden teenager and she had first met Jett. Back
to the days when she had given him her heart, her soul,

her virginity. And he had only to touch her to send her up in flames.

From being cold with shock, she was now burning with response and could feel the colour heating her cheeks.

'Now can we talk about the dress you will create for my sister?'

Rose knew that everyone was watching, that she was the focus of all eyes, and she knew there was only one answer she could give. He had saved her reputation, her business, and the slam of the door told its own story: that Geraldine had conceded defeat and was on her way out of the room, out of the building—please heaven, out of her life.

She had caught that firm and deliberate emphasis on the word *now* even if no one else had. He knew she had tried so hard to get out of the commission he had proposed. The commission that would mean she would have to work with him, for him, all the time she was planning the dress for his sister. At least it was not for his *bride*.

But she'd been here once before, when Nairo had seemed to be her saviour and turned out to be a threat of danger she had barely escaped. So now had she been rescued or entrapped? Was he offering her freedom and a new security or had he actually caught her tight in some carefully planned and deliberately achieved spider's web? Did he really just want her to design a dress for his sister or was there more to his intervention than that?

Right now it seemed that he was her saviour—at least that was what everyone else would think. And because of everyone else, all those eyes on her, she knew she had no option but to give him the response he wanted.

'Miss Cavalliero?'

The prompt sounded easy, almost gentle, but she had regained enough composure to look into his eyes and easy and gentle were not what she saw there.

What she saw was ice, resolve and the sort of ruthless determination that warned her that if she didn't do as he wanted, then he was more than capable of turning this apparent rescue mission into one of total, devastating destruction.

She had been offered a lifeline as long as she went along with what Nairo Moreno wanted. Her life had been full of problems before, but now it seemed that by escaping one set of difficulties she had landed herself with a whole new adversary. One who she suspected was much more formidable than anyone she'd come up against before.

Out of the frying pan and into the fire. But what else could she do?

'Of course, Señor Moreno...' She forced her stiff lips into what must have looked like the most wooden and unbelievable of smiles. 'I'd be happy to discuss your commission with you.'

CHAPTER THREE

NAIRO MIGHT HAVE said that he wanted to discuss the design for his sister's wedding dress, but he showed no inclination to deal with that business right then and there. Instead he waited, smiling, courteous—apparently patient—while Rose spoke to the women who wanted to talk to her about designing their dresses, or their daughters'. The endorsement that Nairo Moreno had given her was apparently enough to convince them that Scarlett was the designer that everyone wanted now.

Which was not surprising really, Rose admitted to herself. After all, as she had discovered earlier in a quick, mind-blowing search on the Internet, the wedding that he was organising for his sister was to be the society event of the year. Esmeralda Roja Moreno was to marry into powerful Austrian aristocracy, it seemed. Duke Oscar Schlieburg was the eldest son of Prince Leopold of Magstein and his wedding was to be almost a state occasion. Her head was spinning simply at the thought of the boost of publicity and the prestige that would come to her business as a result of her involvement with such an event.

A boost that had already started, it seemed, as she collected up the lists of names and addresses of all the potential new customers she'd gained.

'That seemed to be a success,' Nairo's cool voice drawled as the last customer went out the door.

'Success is an understatement.'

Her response came faintly. She had been so absorbed in the matter in hand that she hadn't really been aware of the fact that he had been there all the time, a silent observer, sitting on the edge of the runway, his long black-clad frame standing out so starkly from the white and silver décor. She'd been fooling herself, of course, if she'd let herself think that he had gone. He had set this response in progress with his intervention for his own personal reasons, and now he was going to claim what he felt he was owed.

A chill breeze seemed to blow across Rose's skin as he dropped down from his place on the runway and started towards her and she wished everyone hadn't left her quite so alone.

'Th-thank you for your help. I really appreciate it.'

His dark head nodded, bronze eyes hooded to hide any emotion he might feel.

'There is a price for my assistance.'

Of course there was. This was Nairo Moreno she was dealing with now. A man who had somehow built himself up from the shabby, broken beginnings of their lives when they had first met and who now was this powerful, wealthy man. There had to be a price on anything he did. He was no longer Jett, the youth she had run out on so long ago.

'A price?'

'Oh, don't look so panicked,' he mocked as she turned uncertain eyes on him. 'I'm not going to demand your body in return for my favours in some odd modern version of *droit du seigneur*.'

He paused just long enough for her skin to smart under the bite of his mockery.

'There wouldn't be much point, would there? After all, *we've* already been there, haven't we, *querida*?'

The pointed reminder that they had once been lovers, that he had been the one to take her virginity all those years before, drained the strength from her muscles, making her grab at a nearby chair for support. An innocence that then she had relinquished happily and unhesitatingly, she had been so much under the sway of the heated hunger she had known for this man, blinded to anything but her need for him.

'Been there, done that—didn't bother to stay around to get the tee shirt,' she flashed at him, then immediately regretted her too-aggressive tone.

He might have stepped in to save her business earlier this evening, but what he had decided so surprisingly to give her, he could take away in the blink of an eye. Just as so many new customers had followed his lead to want to use her services, they could easily follow him *away* from her again if he chose to reject her after all.

She must not forget that she was no longer dealing with the Jett of ten years before. This man was a very different sort of male. Tall and powerful, his broad frame had filled out and strengthened where Jett had had a whipcord leanness that had been defined even further by the fact that there was never quite enough to eat in the squat.

Added to that he was someone else entirely—a man of status, with power and money no object. He had a sister who was marrying into the aristocracy and an estate which, if the Internet reports were to be believed, was more than the equal of his prospective in-laws. How he had come by that she had no idea; she didn't want to think about it too closely. She had bitter memories of the appalling ways he had planned on acquiring more money ten years before. But it all added up to someone who was light years away from the scrawny, long-haired Jett she had once believed herself in love with.

Thank heaven she was well over that particular nasty infection! But the scars the past had left on her soul reminded her that she would do best to play this particular game very carefully. Every instinct warned her that Nairo Moreno played to win and that he would prove a spectacular opponent if she was foolish enough to challenge him too far.

'*Querida*...' she echoed cynically. 'How come you're suddenly living in Spain and tossing about Spanish endearments?'

'Not suddenly,' Nairo corrected flatly. 'I always did live in Spain—or, rather, my family home was in Andalusia. And so, naturally, I grew up speaking Spanish.'

'You never used Spanish when we— In the squat.'

'No.' There was even less emotion in the response this time if it was possible. 'I didn't. But then I didn't want anyone there to know who I was.'

Shockingly the fact that he included her in the 'anyone' he hadn't wanted to know the truth about his background, combined with the fact that he had only ever used his native language to her in the brutally sarcastic way he had said *querida* just now, stung at her deep inside.

'And obviously neither did you. So tell me, when did "Red Brown" become the much more exotically named Rose Cavalliero?'

The room suddenly felt chill, as if the heating had been turned off, as from a shadowy corner of her mind came the echo of her mother's voice on the day she had been called to the hospital to find Joy recovering from a brutal beating that Fred Brown had given her.

'My own fault, darling,' Joy had admitted. 'I was a

sucker for a handsome face, a sexy body, a promise of support…and I thought he'd change.'

Wasn't that how it had been with her daughter when Rose had met Nairo?

'Rose was always my given name,' she responded stiffly. 'It's just that Brown was the name I'd been going by—my stepfather's name. You know why I was more than happy to change that when I found I could. It was only when I reunited with my mother and we started talking—really talking—that she told me my father had been an Italian artist she met on holiday—his name was Enzo Cavalliero.'

Another of the good-looking men her mother had fallen for, only to find herself abandoned when things got tougher. Joy had tried to contact him when she'd found herself pregnant, but he'd never responded.

'I've used it ever since. But I don't think that you should throw stones, Señor Moreno. You weren't exactly forthcoming about your true background either.'

A slight inclination of his head was all the acknowledgement of the hit she'd made he was prepared to give.

'Jett was a nickname the gang in the house gave me. It was easier to stick with that.'

But Rose didn't want to linger on the past. The present had enough complications of its own to be dealt with.

'So what exactly is your help going to cost me?' she asked now, determined not to let him see that anything he'd said had had any effect on her.

She was sure that he had expected she would want to know why he had never told anyone the truth about his background and that by deliberately not asking any such thing she had frustrated and irritated him in equal measure.

'More than designing a dress for your sister, I mean.'

A lot more, the hard twist to his mouth warned. But his answer was not what she'd expected.

'I expect you to come and live with me for a month— Oh, not in that way…'

That twist became more pronounced, mocking the startled reaction he had deliberately provoked and that she had been fool enough to give him.

'I doubt that either of us would care to go back to the way things used to be. No—you will come to Spain with me, meet Esmeralda, get to know her properly. You'll work with her on the details of the wedding—the bridesmaids' dresses, the pages' outfits… Everything.'

'I can't manage that,' Rose put in hastily, thankful that there was at least a real excuse for her not to fit in with his plans. She had no wish to spend any more time with him than she absolutely had to. If she had to design his sister's dress, then she would—she had too much to lose if she didn't. But the swirl of personal memories threatened to put her completely off balance and she desperately wanted to get this back onto a purely business level.

'I was telling the truth when I said that my mother is unwell.'

The way his dark brows snapped together warned her of what was coming and she knew the question was one she would have wanted answering for herself. Nairo had been the only other person she'd confided in about her stepfather's abuse and, worse, he also knew that Joy had sided with her husband in the face of Rose's accusations. That was why she had run away, a desperate move that had ended by throwing her into the arms of the man who had called himself Jett.

At that time Nairo had understood unquestioningly. That was one of the reasons she'd fallen head over heels for him, wildly, crazily, until she'd learned her lesson. She was secretly stunned that he even remembered, never mind felt some of the anger he had showed then.

'And you'd put your life on hold, ruin your business for her?'

When she had done nothing of the sort for her daughter. The implication was there and Rose knew she couldn't deny it. It was the way she had felt herself and it had taken long years of distance and slow, painful reconciliation before she had managed to reach the place she was in now.

'She's my mother.'

He was obviously not convinced.

'And did she act like a mother when she took your stepfather's side against you?' There was something new and shockingly savage in his tone so that Rose had to hurry to reassure him.

'She regretted that deeply. She was scared—terrified. She'd been a single mother once and found it so hard. No money, no support.'

So Joy had thought her salvation lay in the support of a man, any man. And she was, as she had admitted, a sucker for a handsome face. Fred Brown had been a very good-looking man. A handsome face that hid a personality as black as pitch. But admitting that took Rose down paths she didn't want to follow as they reminded her that at one point—more than one—she had found herself to be very much her mother's daughter.

'But when I found her again she was in a real mess. Brown had been treating her as a punchbag because he was so angry I'd got away from him.'

'Is that what's wrong with her now?'

'No—she had breast cancer. She had the operation and now she's recovering from treatment. She's getting better every day, but I wouldn't feel right about leaving her even…'

'Then I'll make sure that she has the very best care.' Nairo dismissed her objection with a wave of his hand. 'A live-in nurse—anything and everything she needs.'

Just the thought of Joy having professional care, the attention that Rose hadn't been able to devote to her and run the wedding boutique as well, brought such a rush of relief that she almost grabbed the offer right out of his hands. She'd felt so guilty at the way she'd had to neglect her mother recently, leaving her in the tiny flat for far too many hours on her own. The demands of just scraping a living, finding the money to keep a roof over their heads, had forced her to focus on her work far more than she'd liked and it had given her an insight into why her mother had been prepared to grasp at anything—anyone—who seemed to offer an alternative. But the uneasy, apprehensive feeling that came with wondering why he was offering—and demanding—so much forced her to hesitate.

'I don't usually work this way!'

Everything was happening too fast. Only yesterday she had been barely aware that Nairo Moreno even existed, let alone that he was actually the boy she had once given her naïve foolish heart to, all grown up and turned into this unstoppable masculine force.

'It's this way or no way,' Nairo retorted.

'And if I don't agree?'

'I reckon Geraldine would be able to point me in the direction of another designer.'

It was said so lightly, even carelessly, that she couldn't believe he meant it. But meeting his stony eyes told a very different story. He meant every word and if he did go elsewhere, with Geraldine's recommendation, then her business was dead in the water. Her reputation would be shredded for ever if it got out that Nairo Moreno had withdrawn his commission from her.

'But why can't your sister come here and talk things over with me? That's how I usually work—how it would be with any other client.'

'Esmeralda is not just any other client. This wedding has to be perfect, and my sister has to have everything she wants.'

She sounded like a spoiled little princess and already Rose was regretting having anything to do with this wedding. Yet how could she regret taking on the commission that might turn her life around? If the response to Nairo's announcement that she was to design Esmeralda's dress was anything to go by, once this commission was completed, then surely everyone would forget the cancelled wedding, the 'broken-hearted' groom left almost at the altar? She would put her heart and soul into creating the most beautiful gown for Nairo's sister so that the wedding would be the perfect showcase for what she could design in the future.

How long would it take? A month, he'd said. Maybe less? She could cope with that, couldn't she? After all, she probably wouldn't have to see Nairo himself for any real amount of that time. He was a man, and from her experience the males involved in weddings, even the most doting grooms, stayed well back for as much of the time as they could.

'You'd really make sure that my mother has a nurse?'

'If that is what it takes. A live-in carer in attendance twenty-four hours a day. I know of an agency...'

Nairo named an exclusive and highly rated agency, the sort of establishment with fees that Rose couldn't even dream of being able to afford.

'You can choose her yourself—I'll set up the interviews for tomorrow if that will suit you.'

It would more than suit. It was far more than she could

ever have anticipated. If only it hadn't been Nairo who was behind it all. Surely he couldn't want her that much.

But of course. She almost laughed aloud. *He* didn't want *her*. He was here at the bidding of his sister. That demanding little princess.

'I understand how you feel about leaving your mother,' Nairo put in unexpectedly. 'My sister has been ill too. That is why she is not here with me.'

'Oh. I'm sorry to hear that.'

A kick of guilt left Rose feeling uncomfortable. She should be grateful to Esmeralda; because of his sister Nairo was offering her a lifeline that she had never anticipated.

'I'll look forward to working with her on the designs for her wedding—to make her dream dress, for a perfect day.'

'I'd appreciate that, thank you,' he said, his voice unexpectedly rough at the edges, and something had changed in Nairo's face. A relaxation of the muscles in his jaw, an unexpected light in his eyes, turning Rose's feelings upside down. She didn't care if the concern was all for his sister, only knew that the sudden rush of release from the tensions of the past year or more had gone to her head like the prosecco she had served earlier that evening.

'No, thank *you*!'

Her head spun with such relief it pushed into an unguarded response and before she had quite realised what she was doing she had come up close and pressed her lips against his cheek.

A kiss of thanks. That was all it was meant to be. Just a peck on the cheek. There and gone again in a minute. But as soon as her lips touched his skin, felt its warmth and the hardness of bone beneath her mouth, the moment the taste of him touched her lips she knew that it wouldn't stay that way. It couldn't end there.

It was like putting a match to a drift of dried tinder deep

inside her, setting everything burning, making her control crack dangerously. She remembered what that taste had been like before, what a simple kiss had led to. Something so wild, so passionate that it had been impossible to control. It was reaching out to grab hold of her already, turning her blood white-hot, melting her bones so that she swayed on her feet. She would have fallen if Nairo hadn't reached out and grabbed both her arms, holding her upright. Holding her close.

'Red...' Nairo said roughly, and the rawness in his voice told its own story. One she wanted and yet feared to hear.

It was still there. The sparks that flashed like lightning when they looked at each other, the flames that flared if they touched. She'd felt it in that moment when he had touched her cheek in the shop doorway and it was bubbling up inside her now like lava in a volcano, threatening to spill out and swamp her in a scalding flood.

'Rose...'

The fact that he had corrected her name only seemed to make matters worse. His tone was tight, constricted as if he was having trouble getting words out of his throat. But then he gave up on even trying. The proud dark head bent swiftly, his mouth coming down on hers in a hard, bruising kiss. It crushed her lips back against her teeth, opening them to allow the stroke of his tongue, tasting her, tantalising her. She could barely snatch in a breath under the pressure of his kiss as she let her head fall back, opening to him so that he could plunder her mouth. Time evaporated, sweeping all memories before it, and in her thoughts she was once more back in the scruffy darkness of the squat, alone with this man who had come to her rescue when she had most needed him, and who had stolen her naïve heart as a result.

The ten years in between had vanished. She was once

more the girl she had been then, young, innocent, lost in a world of sensation that she had never known existed.

Something she hadn't experienced since in all the time between.

It was like opening a door and letting in the sunshine. Nairo's strength was a powerful support, one she still needed as she swayed against him again. Her arms came up, reaching for him once more...

'No!' he said harshly, wrenching his mouth away, shocking her out of her dream world.

It had been a dream then too. Like the sort of fairy tale her mother had been looking for. She had thought him her rescuer, but she hadn't known the truth.

The long body so close to hers had frozen, stiff and taut. She could feel him staring down at her even though she couldn't see it, and she had to force her eyes open to meet his.

The darkness of desire had changed his eyes, distending his pupils so that there was only the faintest gold at their rim, and yet, in spite of that one betraying reaction, he couldn't have been further from her if he had been on the opposite side of the world.

His hands clamped hard and tight around her shoulders, pushing her away, the ferocity of rejection in his movements.

'No!' He didn't need the extra emphasis. His feelings were perfectly clear. 'This isn't going to happen. It isn't what I want.'

Liar! The word sounded in Rose's head and she wanted to throw it at him, to challenge him with it. The way her body was stinging in response to that kiss screamed at her to defy his hard-voiced declaration. How could he say that when she had felt his reaction in the tightness of his body, could still see it shadowing his eyes?

But even as her mouth opened to speak she caught the word back, swallowed it down, knowing that it was safer that way. But she wasn't going to let him get away unchallenged.

'My, you do have a tendency to overreact, don't you?' she tossed at him. 'It was just a little kiss.'

'Some *little* kiss.'

Nairo couldn't stop his mouth from quirking up into a smile at her response as he recognised her repetition of the comment he had turned on her in the boutique earlier. She had spirit, he'd give her that. But 'a little kiss' went no way towards describing what they'd just shared. A little kiss wasn't possible between them.

The taste of her was still on his tongue, his lips. His senses burned and every nerve still throbbed from the response that had blazed its way through him. The heat and hardness below his belt made it impossible to think straight. But when he looked into her eyes he knew he *had* to think straight. Hell, someone had to or he would give in to the primitive demands of his body that screamed for appeasement, throwing her down on the thickly carpeted floor, crushing her under his weight.

She would let him, he knew that without a doubt. She might scratch and hiss like an angry kitten, but she could not deny the enticement, the welcome that had been there in her eyes, in her touch—in that far from *little* kiss.

'However little it was, it's not what I want from you.'

'I should hope not, because that's not what I want from you either.'

She might try to disguise the flinch away from his words, bring her head up a little bit higher to declare defiance and rejection, but she was still fighting a disappointment that was every bit as strong as the one that was biting at him. The wide, blurred pupils gave away the fact that she was as turned on as he was. Even after ten years he still remembered how she looked when she was aroused and hungry for the pleasure he could give her.

'I might sign up to design your sister's dress—but that's all. It's a business deal, nothing more.'

'A business deal suits me fine,' Nairo echoed with a curt nod, holding out his hand to her.

She took it, even clasped it firmly and shook it in a very businesslike manner, but not before he'd noted the hesitation, the tiny jerk of her fingers as his palm touched hers. He knew just what that meant. Hell, wasn't he feeling it too? How could he miss the way her tongue slipped out, slicked across dry lips, the forced way she swallowed against an obviously tight throat?

He could have her right now if he wanted, and— *querido Dios*—he *wanted*. The need was like a searing brand on his body. He wanted her and he could have her if he just pressed a little more…kissed her again…caressed her…

He could have her, but what good would this be if, after all this time, after ten years' waiting, it was fast and furious, totally uncontrolled?

The demanding pulse that had taken prisoner of his senses insisted that it would be worth it—*right now*. But the little part of his brain that was still rational told another story. One that offered a fuller, deeper satisfaction.

Waiting would be worth it. Waiting would build the hunger, the sense of need, in her as well as himself. If he kept her waiting, then he would keep her hungry. The hungrier she became, the more complete his triumph would be when he finally made her his. This time she wouldn't be able to walk away from him.

This time he would be the one doing the walking.

'Can I give you a lift home?' It wasn't easy to make it sound careless, relaxed.

Her head came up, eyes wary at even that simple question.

'No, thank you. I still have some tidying up to do here. And I have a taxi coming...'

'Then I'll see you tomorrow—for the interviews. I'll call the agency and set them up.'

'That would be perfect.'

Her smile was a fake flash on and off, not meeting her eyes, not warming her face in the slightest. She might think that she was showing nothing, but he knew Rose Cavalliero, as he must now call her, of old. The harder she worked to project the fact that she was feeling nothing, the more she had to conceal.

It wouldn't be a problem keeping her wanting. He'd seen the disappointment in her eyes when he'd pulled back. It had almost been worth the difficulty he'd had to wrench his lips away from the warm, soft invitation of hers just to see the way those mossy-green eyes clouded with disbelief and frustration. The fire that had flamed between them all those years ago was still there, totally undimmed by ten years' absence. If anything, it was stronger now. The desire of a grown man for a woman rather than the adolescent rush of hormones he had known before. He had thought that he had wanted her then, but it was nothing compared to what he felt now.

'Tomorrow, then.'

Not a man to let grass grow under his feet, this Nairo Moreno, Rose reflected as she made herself take the business card he passed her. He had come prepared for this and would allow for no other possible outcome.

If anything should tell her just what his trip to England was really all about, it was that. All her earlier fears, the secret thrill of dread that he might actually have come looking for her after all this time, evaporated in a hiss that almost sounded like laughter at her own stupidity.

She couldn't have been more deluded.

He didn't want her. He couldn't have made that any plainer if he'd tried. The flat, emphatic statement left no room for doubt. He didn't want her and that should have made things so much easier. She should feel relieved, because she was going to have to travel to Spain with him, to stay there for a month while she worked on his sister's dress, and it would be so much easier knowing that she meant nothing to him, that he didn't want her in any way.

So why, instead of the relief she should feel, the soar of elation and freedom, was the emotion that filled her built on the sort of disappointment that shrivelled her heart?

CHAPTER FOUR

'You NEED TO tell me about the wedding.'

'What?'

Rose lifted her head from the sketches she was concentrating on to see Nairo standing in the doorway of the workroom that had been set apart for her in the Castillo Corazón. This was the first time that he had approached her since they had arrived at his magnificent family home, and she'd been grateful for his absence as she tried to get her head round what had happened to her.

It seemed that in the time since Nairo Moreno had appeared in her life her world had been turned upside down. Was it really possible that it was less than a week since that moment and yet she seemed to have lost control of her life as surely as if someone—Nairo obviously—had wrenched the reins from her hands and was directing things the way that *he* wanted.

Nairo didn't wait for anything, it seemed. He wanted a carer for Rose's mother—one had been selected, appointed, moved into the tiny flat that she and her daughter shared, while Rose was whisked off to the airport in a chauffeured car, escorted onto a sleek private jet and transported here to Andalusia, where the luxurious golden-walled *castillo* was to be her base for the next four weeks or so. It felt as if she had been transported into a different world instead of just to another part of Europe. Her work-room alone, opening out onto a Moorish-style patio, would have swallowed up more than half of the shabby little flat that she had struggled to pay rent on and the suite she had been installed in with its tiled floors and decorated ceiling was almost twice the size of her London boutique.

When she had first seen her room, it had been like going back in time, with the huge canopied bed and the rather old-fashioned furnishings giving the place a for-mal, rather stiff, dark look. The most wonderful aspect of the room was the wide balcony overlooking the gardens and the river below. But she didn't have time to explore, to enjoy the beauty of her surroundings or even have a swim in the large outdoor pool. She was here to do a job and it was so much easier if she focussed on that and nothing else. It would also mean that she could get out of here as soon as possible.

'I didn't think that you'd be interested. But here...'

'Not that.'

Nairo waved away the pages covered with designs and colour swatches she held out to him.

'Not Esmeralda's wedding—I understand that that is going fine. No, I meant the wedding that never was—the one you were supposed to have with Lord what's-his-name...'

'Andrew,' Rose supplied flatly.

'Yes, Lord Andrew Holden. The man you supposedly left at the altar on the day of the wedding.'

'Three days before the wedding, actually.'

Rose knew she sounded snappy when really she was fighting with the rush of tension that stretched each mus-cle tight as she answered him. The thought of the day she had realised she couldn't go through with her wedding was particularly uncomfortable with Nairo before her, reminding her of the memories that had driven her to make that decision.

'Why do you want to know?'

'Because Oscar and his parents are getting concerned.'

Rose had seen Nairo's prospective in-laws, the Prince and Grand Duchess, only once, but that was enough to make her understand exactly why he was so insistent that things would be perfect for them. Their emphasis on propriety and social esteem meant that they would expect nothing less. And it was obvious that Nairo's sister was very much in awe of them.

From the moment that she had met Esmeralda Moreno she'd understood even more. Nairo's sister was almost nine years younger than him and, while she shared his black-haired, golden-eyed colouring, she had nothing of his powerful build and strength. Instead she was tiny, delicate, finely built. Too thin and nervy, speaking too quickly, worrying about too much. Rose suspected that she showed signs of suffering from some sort of eating disorder in the past, which made it clear why Nairo was so concerned and protective.

Esmeralda was definitely not the spoiled princess she had anticipated but a vulnerable woman who desperately wanted people to like her. And Rose did like her, very much.

'Oh, come on, I'm only the dress designer!' she protested. 'When the big day arrives, I'll be out of here and gone.'

She sincerely hoped that would be the case. Living here like this with Nairo likely to appear at any moment was stretching her nerves so tight she felt they might actually snap. It should have been an easy matter to avoid him in the huge *castillo*, but somehow she always seemed to bump into him when she least expected it. She was beginning to feel like a hunted animal, on high alert at every moment, while Nairo was perfectly polite but totally indifferent and businesslike.

This isn't going to happen, he had said and it seemed that he was determined to keep to that.

Still she found herself tensing up whenever Nairo walked into a room, focussing so hard on what she was doing that it was almost a discomfort. She was so aware of him, of the lean length of his tall dark figure, the glint of the sun on the rich darkness of his hair, the beautifully accented sound of his voice, the scent of his skin blended with a tempting citrus cologne. It was only then that she realised how deep she had dug a gaping hole at her feet and foolishly allowed herself to fall into it. She had fallen back into the bonds of his physical spell as badly as she had done all those years before, when she had been just an adolescent, and every day she spent at the Castillo Corazón pulled those bonds tighter and harder around her, stopping her from thinking straight and from sleeping at night.

She couldn't even use her mother as an excuse. The nurse that Nairo had provided for Joy had proved to be perfection in a human form. 'My guardian angel' her mother called her and under the woman's gentle care Rose's mother had not only been more comfortable than she had ever been when Rose had struggled with her care as well as running the boutique, she had actually thrived. The two women had become great friends so that as well as providing her medical care, Margaret also gave Joy the sort of female companionship she had been longing for. The sort of friendship that, try as she might, Rose had never been able to really have with her parent. There were too many shadows between them. Margaret and Joy shared knitting patterns, read books, enjoyed cooking together and Rose knew that she would be going a long way towards risking the steady progress of her convalescence if she was to take Margaret away.

There was more to it too. The last time she'd spoken to her mother there had been a new, very different note in Joy's voice. One she hadn't heard in so long—if ever at all. Pushed to describe it, she'd have had to say that there was a lack of the guilt that had always been just under the surface ever since they had reunited when Rose had gone to visit her in the hospital after Fred's last attack on her.

They'd determined to put the past behind them, made a home together, but Rose knew that her mother's conscience always troubled her when she looked back, particularly when she'd seen how hard her daughter worked to keep the roof over their heads. So now the relief and delight at what she saw as Rose's newfound success lightened every word, every phrase. After all the time it had taken them to rebuild their relationship, could she really risk going back on that?

'It's not as simple as that,' Nairo said now. 'There has already been a lot of interest in the fact that you're here—and involved in Esmeralda's wedding. I need to know how to handle it if the paparazzi come hanging round the gates, trying to take photographs. There's a risk that they're becoming more interested in *you* than the bride and groom and they're starting to demand to know whether you're a curse on any wedding you're involved with.'

'Oh, that's just stupid and you know it.'

Rose used the need to put the papers back into order and down onto the table as a defence against the rush of colour she knew had heated her cheeks.

'I saw the effect just the mention of the story had on the audience at your fashion show,' Nairo stated coolly. 'It could have turned pretty nasty.'

'Because Geraldine stirred it up. She won't be here at Esmeralda's wedding.'

'But you will be, and if you come trailing the shadows of your past life behind you and bring the paparazzi to our door, then it will turn this whole thing into an ordeal for my sister instead of the happiest day of her life.'

'Well, you should have thought of that when you asked me to design the dress for her and made sure that I would do it.'

You have a nerve to talk about past scandals, Rose wanted to fling in his face, but the memories of how she too was connected to that past dried the words on her tongue. Combining those memories with the thought of her mother's happiness and health now made sure that she didn't dare risk opening another can of worms. She couldn't forget the unspoken threat that had been in his warning that she was not to talk to anyone about the time when they had met before.

Echoes of that time had surfaced on the first day when they had reached the *castillo.* As she had got out of the car, Rose had stared up at the huge, beautiful golden building, with the darkening rays of the setting sun vividly reflected in the glass of every wide-paned window.

'Is all this yours?' she'd gasped, unable to believe it. Unable to connect this glorious, elegant building with the man she had first known to be living in a squat, no job, no money of his own.

'It is now,' Nairo had responded flatly. 'I inherited from my father. What?'

He'd looked down at her sharply.

'You don't think all this is bought with the profits from my dirty dealing?'

It was the first time he had breached the wall of silence they had built around the past. The wall she had had to build around it in order to be able to go on with this 'business arrangement'.

'I never…' she'd begun, but at that moment the great wooden door of the *castillo* had opened and a tiny whirlwind in the shape of his sister, Esmeralda, had rushed out to meet them, flinging herself into Nairo's arms and hugging him tightly so that there had been no chance of continuing the conversation.

It still hung there between them now, unspoken, not dealt with, and Rose knew that one day it would have to be faced or it would blight the rest of her life.

'You saw enough to realise that I have a "past",' she flung at him. 'That was the time to get out of things if you'd wanted to keep this squeaky clean so as not to offend your in-laws. Instead you made sure that I got this commission and that everyone there knew it. Why?'

It was a question he'd asked himself so many times, Nairo acknowledged. If he'd had any sense, he should have turned and left her to the ruin of her fledgling business. He'd have found another designer to please Esmeralda. He'd have appeased his sister somehow and not jumped, feet first, into the murky puddle of complications and memories that this woman brought with her. But, Esmeralda or not, he had known from the start that he couldn't just turn and walk away from her. Not until he'd got her well and truly out of his system.

'You were the designer Esmeralda wanted. And I hate bullies. Geraldine was a born bully, anyone could see that. She wanted the attention to herself and she was determined to do anything to win it. I enjoyed making sure she didn't succeed.'

It was true he hated bullies, and he had no trouble recognising an emotional tormenter when he saw one. Hadn't he seen enough with the way his young stepmother had treated Esmeralda, whom she'd considered a rival for her husband's affections? Though he'd never reckoned that she would start on him as well. That was why he had moved forward to act when Geraldine had been trying to stir up trouble. But there was more to it than that. In spite of everything, the memory of the way Rose had walked away from him, in spite of the fact that the tall, elegant woman who stood on the runway in that clinging peacock-blue dress was light years from the girl he'd befriended and protected in the squat, he had still seen some faint and unexpected traces of the Red he had known back then. He'd seen the stress lines round her eyes, the way she was biting her lower lip. The memory had disturbed his responses so sharply that he had moved forward, acted, spoken, before he had even realised what he was doing.

'She was supposed to be marrying Andrew before he met me. She wanted her revenge.'

'I would have thought she'd have been happier to have him back on the market.'

'Mmm.' Rose looked uncomfortable about that. 'The problem was that he didn't want her back. He'd been looking for an excuse to break off with her and—well, I provided it.'

'Are you saying he didn't love you?'

'No.' Bright auburn hair caught the blaze of the sun as she shook her head, sending it flying in the air. It also sent the aroma of her perfume, light and delicate, wafting towards him, threatening to scramble his thoughts so that he had to drag them back into focus. 'The opposite. He was crazy about me.'

The emphasis on the word *crazy* warned him there was more to this story than she was happy to acknowledge.

'So what happened? Why did you call the wedding off? He was too "crazy"?'

And Nairo was too aware, Rose reflected secretly. He'd caught on some betraying note in her voice, a look in her eyes, and seen part of what she would have liked to have kept hidden from him.

'He was...rather obsessed,' she managed, finding it embarrassing to say any such thing to this man. Why would he believe that Andrew had been so over the top in his avowals of devotion and adoration when Nairo himself had found her so totally forgettable? 'I—I realised that I didn't feel the way that he did. He took it badly.'

'Three days before the wedding,' Nairo murmured darkly.

'I know! I know! You can't make me feel any worse than I do already.' She'd lived with the guilt ever since.

Her voice sounded too uneven, too raw, and she had to move away, riffling through the papers in her hand as if looking for something special amongst them. There was no way she was going to admit that she had tried so hard to care for Andrew as he'd wanted. She knew there was no great passion between them; they hadn't even made love. But she had thought that would all come in time. Until the day when, sorting out her belongings, ready for the move to the elegant apartment that was to be her new home, she'd come across a dusty, faded box at the back of a cupboard.

In that box had been the one and only photograph of herself with Nairo she had ever owned. Creased and battered, it was one of a set they had taken in a cheap photo booth on an afternoon when they had actually had a few pounds to spare. A joyful, laughter-filled day that she had wanted to record for ever and so had dragged Nairo into the booth with her in spite of his protests.

The sketches in front of her blurred now just as that photograph had done then and she blinked hard. How could she have married Andrew—married anyone—when she knew she didn't feel anything like the overwhelming power of emotion that had swept over her when she had been with the man she had known as Jett? She couldn't have given herself to anyone else unless she had felt something that had at least come close to what she had felt then. The man she still felt that way about, she realised with a feeling that left her fighting for breath.

Even worse, she knew she had proved herself to be her mother's daughter when she'd rushed in without thought, just as Joy had plunged into marriage to Fred Brown. She'd believed she'd found someone who would care for her, someone who would take the burdens from the shoulders that had supported them since she'd promised to help her mother escape from her stepfather's brutal influence. In a weak moment she'd seen hope and so she'd said yes, only to realise that she'd done so for the worst possible reasons.

'I should never have said yes to his proposal. Our engagement was a terrible mistake.'

'Why such a mistake?' Nairo questioned. 'Looking at it from the outside, I would have thought that Andrew Holden was the perfect choice.'

'Oh, really? And why was that?'

He'd caught her on the raw there, he could hear it in her voice as she tossed the question over her shoulder at him, the muscles in her face stiff and tight with rejection.

'Good-looking, tall, successful, with a great position in society. Wealthy...'

That brought her spinning round to face him. Her eyes were unusually bright as she turned them on his face.

'And you think that his money was the answer to everything? The reason why I wanted to marry him in the first place?'

Nairo shrugged indifferently, brushing off her challenge to him.

'Isn't that what women want in a marriage?'

It was what his mother and stepmother had wanted from his father. The old man had always been a sucker for a pretty face, a sexy body. He had been so convinced that he was 'in love' that the thought of a prenup had never entered his head. Between them, his two wives had drained almost everything the old man had to offer and then headed for pastures new when there was nothing left. The first Señora Moreno had been happy to leave her children behind, not wanting her pleasurable lifestyle with her new partner to be restricted by a son and daughter, then just nine and one year old. The second, Carmen, had even tried to take Raoul's son from him in the end.

He'd vowed that he would never leave himself as vulnerable to any woman as his father had done, and for most of his life he had kept to that vow. The only reason he had ever come close to breaking it was standing before him now. He'd had a lucky escape there. One that had taught him a much-needed lesson on the risks of weakening. At least he had had the sense to keep the truth about his family from her, though he'd come close to telling her that Christmas when he'd tried for a reconciliation with his father. She'd still found a way to make money out of their relationship when she'd gone to the police.

'Not me!'

The fury of her indignation clashed with his own challenging stare so that he could almost see the spark where they met in the air between them.

'But your business was in difficulties—you're oceans deep in debt.'

That made her head go back, green eyes widening in shock.

'How do you know that?'

The smile he couldn't hold back wouldn't have looked

friendly. It wasn't meant to. It was just an on-off twitch of muscles, an uncontrolled response to the realisation that even now she still didn't recognise the difference between the raw youth he'd been and the man he was now.

'I make it my business to know everything about anyone I'm dealing with. If I want the information, it's easy enough to get it. So wouldn't marriage to him have solved all your money problems?'

'Maybe—yes. But shouldn't the fact that I *didn't* marry him show you that that wasn't what I was looking for from him?'

He had to concede that, Nairo acknowledged. But if that was not the reason she'd been prepared to marry this Andrew, then why had she backed out so late? For an uncomfortable moment he was back at the fashion show, watching the woman called Geraldine brandishing the newspaper with the scandalous headline right in Rose's face. He'd stepped forward to stop the obvious attack right then and there, but he'd never actually really challenged himself on *why* he'd done that. He'd claimed that he hated bullies— and he did—and the sight of her pale, strained face had taken him back ten years to the moment when he'd first set eyes on her looking lost and alone on a London street.

But there was more to it than that.

'Wouldn't I be much more comfortable, more settled, as Lady Holden?'

'As I recall, you always dreamed of marriage and a happy-ever-after...'

He let the rest of the sentence fade off into a dark growl, not liking the memories that came pushing to the surface as he spoke.

I don't do love. I don't do commitment... Through the years his own voice came back to haunt him. He'd been so sure, looking at the ruins of his father's two marriages, the destruction they'd left behind—particularly for Esmeralda. *I certainly don't do marriage. If you want those, then you'd better find yourself someone who does.*

But the irony was that in the moment that Geraldine's announcement had made him realise Rose had done exactly that—found someone else, agreed to marry him—then his world had rocked off balance and he'd found himself moving forward, taking action without really thinking things through.

It hadn't even been the fact that he wanted to please Esmeralda. This went deeper, was more personal than that. He didn't want Rose being with anyone else. He wanted this woman back in his life, in his bed.

He hadn't had enough of her ten years ago and he didn't intend letting her be with anyone else until he'd got her out of his system.

'Perhaps I did,' Rose acknowledged. 'But there would have been no happy-ever-after. I was very fond of him, but I could never give him what he needed from me. My timing was really really bad, but it would have been far worse if I'd married him and then realised my mistake.'

It all sounded so perfectly rational, so believeable. At least, it would have been if it hadn't been for the way that her eyes wouldn't quite meet his. She was holding something back, hiding something from him. But before he could try to drag out of her just what it was, the door opened and his sister hurried into the room.

'So have you finished your sketches, Rose?' she asked, her voice bubbling with excitement. 'Have you got something to show me?'

'Yes, I have them here…'

Rose reached for the sketches from the table once again and it was only now that he saw how much her grip on them had been crumpling the paper so that she had to smooth them out to show Esmeralda her designs.

'If we've finished…'

Her hazel eyes went to Nairo's face, her eyebrows lifting in question. He knew what she was asking, what put that faint frown of concern between her fine dark brows. Was he going to leave things there, with whatever she'd kept hidden still unsaid?

It seemed he was going to have to because her question, the look she turned on him, alerted his sister to his presence in the room.

'I didn't see you there, big brother! Don't tell me you've suddenly developed an interest in bridesmaids' dresses—because that's all we're going to let you have a peek at! No one but Rose and I will see *the* dress before the big day. It's our secret.'

'And that's how you must keep it.'

Rose could only blink in astonishment as she heard the change in Nairo's tone as he addressed his sister. The cold stiffness had melted away, leaving a warmth that flowed over her like liquid honey. But only for Esmeralda. When he turned back to her his eyes were opaque and hooded, hiding any emotion.

'Would I dare to get in Esmeralda's way?' he drawled. 'We're finished here—for now. We can carry on this converation at another time.'

So was that a promise or a threat? Rose had no way of knowing because as he finished speaking Nairo moved to drop a quick, affectionate kiss on his sister's head, then strolled out the door. The gentle gesture wrenched at her heart, reminding her of how she had once believed that he had cared for her too.

No—bitter realism made her add it as the door began to swing to behind Nairo's tall figure. Gentleness and warmth were not what there had ever been between the two of them. Their relationship had been based on a searing sexual passion that had caught them up in a conflagration too wild, too ferocious to be resisted. She might have thought there was concern at first, when he had come up to her when she had been sitting on the stone steps in Trafalgar Square, cold and miserable, too tired to go any further. One of her shoes had split, letting in the wet, and her hair had hung in damp rat's tails around her face and shoulders. Perhaps then he'd felt a touch of concern for her. He couldn't have felt anything else.

Quite frankly, then she'd been a mess.

'So—Rose—do you have the designs—the dress…?' Esmeralda's excited voice broke into her thoughts as she tugged the sheets of paper from her hand. 'Let me see.'

Rose could only be thankful that the younger girl's enthusiasm and excitement meant that she didn't notice her own distraction, the way that her mind was far from focussing on anything like the plans for the wedding dress but instead had followed Nairo out the door and back into the past they had once shared.

'Oh, but these are *gorgeous*! *Maravilloso!* Perhaps we should have let my brother stay and see these. Then he'd understand why I insisted that it had to be you designing my dress and he should fetch you for me.'

She sounded so determined, so resolute that for a moment Rose remembered once again the way she had dismissed Nairo's sister as a spoiled, demanding little princess. But she'd seen with her own eyes since she had come to stay at the *castillo* that Esmeralda was a charmer, a delight. She could easily wind anyone round her delicate fingers, but she only used that appeal on her obviously besotted brother. No one could have missed the way he watched his little sister so closely, a faint frown deepening the lines around his stunning eyes. There was more than just brotherly affection behind that watchfulness. Some memory that it seemed only the two of them shared.

'Surely they would impress even him,' Esmeralda was chattering on, unaware of the way that Rose's thoughts had drifted away. 'They might even convince him that romance really does exist.'

'Your brother is not a romantic?'

By imposing enough control over her voice she managed to make it sound relaxed, even light.

'Surely someone living here amongst all this beauty...' The wave of her hand took in the high decorated ceiling, the tiled floor that led out onto the patio, the sun streaming through the wooden blinds from the garden, where the sound of the river below in the valley was a gentle background song to the formal beauty of the *castillo*. There was so much to the place that she still hadn't seen.

'Oh, *no*...' Esmeralda shook her dark head sharply. 'He has no time for looking at his surroundings, not even to bring this place up to date really. He's had to work too hard to make sure that the estate was saved and that we could still live here.'

'The estate was in danger?'

Seeing the elegant luxury that surrounded her when contrasted with her own small flat, Rose found it hard to believe any such thing.

'We almost lost everything,' Esmeralda assured her. '*Papá* was ill and he let things slide. That was when he brought Nairo back from Argentina after seeing the great job he did there.'

'Argentina?' It was a strangled sound of surprise.

So Nairo had lived abroad for some—how much?— of the time since they had been together in the squat. No wonder he'd seemed to have disappeared off the face of the earth and she had never seen or heard anything of him since that fateful night.

Esmeralda nodded. 'We have an *estancia*. That was almost derelict too. But my brother, he knows how to work—and work.' Her endearing, bright smile quirked her mouth up at the corners. 'Even if *Papá* didn't approve of so much he did out there.'

'No time for romance?' The uncomfortable fluttering of her heart made it a struggle to speak.

'No time—and no *heart* for romance. I'm not quite sure what happened, but I know that when he was in England he met someone.'

Esmeralda shook her head as if in disbelief.

'Some cold, cruel little witch who stamped on his heart and then betrayed him without a care. She got off unscathed, but my brother... Pah! If I could get my hands on her...'

Rose's head was spinning. *When he was in England...* Could Esmeralda mean *her* as the 'cold, cruel little witch'? But that was not how it had been. Nairo had been the one who deserved those accusations. He must have told the story differently.

Nairo had once told her why he was in London, living in the squat. A huge row with his father, so he had just walked out, taking no money with him. 'A woman' had been behind it was all he would say. So did Esmeralda have it wrong and the woman who had hurt her brother was actually someone he'd left behind in Spain?

Or perhaps Rose was too sensitive to this account of things? Perhaps there had been some other woman in England... Unfortunately that version of things didn't bring any sense of relief, only a tangled mess of complicated feelings that twisted and burned at the thought of Nairo

being so involved with someone else that the other woman
had left him feeling that she had 'stamped on his heart'.

Stamped on his heart! That made it obvious that *Rose*
couldn't be the woman Esmeralda had meant. The Nairo
she had known had had no heart to be stamped on.

From the depths of her thoughts a flash of dark memory came back to haunt her. Nairo holding Julie, the girl-
friend of Jason, an older man who also shared the squat,
the blonde woman's head on his shoulder. The burn of jeal-
ousy she had felt had been like nothing she'd ever known.

A faint noise out in the hallway made Rose glance up.
Reflected in the mirror on one wall, she could see the tall
dark figure of Nairo just beyond the doorway almost blending into the shadows of the wooden-panelled corridor beyond. He hadn't walked away at all but must have heard
every word of the last conversation. As her head came up,
she saw the heavy lids that hooded his eyes lift so that he
was staring straight at her.

Just for a moment their eyes locked in the reflection in
the glass, the intensity of his stare making her blood run
cold in her veins. Then he turned on his heel and strode
away.

CHAPTER FIVE

Rose was out on the patio, at work on her designs, the sun gilding her arms exposed by the sleeveless white cotton top. She had pulled her chair right to the edge of the swimming pool and let her bare feet fall into it so that the water lapped against her lightly tanned toes as her head was bent over the sketch pad on her knees. Her pencil moved swiftly and confidently over the paper, adding a flurry of lace here, a waterfall of a train there. Her auburn hair tumbled forward over her face as she concentrated, the copper strands in it caught and illuminated by the setting sun until they glowed a fiery red, much closer to the colour they had been when Nairo had first seen her.

He had been away from the *castillo* for only four days and yet coming back to her now was like seeing her anew.

It had been the red of her hair that he had first seen, spotting her slumped wearily against a wall, the brilliant glow shining out in the dull grey of a wintry afternoon in spite of the fact that it had been raining heavily and her corkscrew curls were limp around her head. Long, thin legs in faded black leggings had been splayed out on the steps she was sitting on as if she didn't have the energy to place them any other way, and her head was down-bent then as it was now, but then it had been a sign of depression and withdrawal, not the current focus on creativity.

He had easily picked her up from the pavement where she sat and carried her when she had swayed against him in obvious weakness. She hadn't eaten for two days, she'd told him later. She'd left home in a frantic rush, running from her abusive stepfather, no time to collect more than her handbag. But her purse had had so little cash in it, and that stepfather had put a stop on the bank card he had once let her have.

A card he had later expected her to pay for with sexual favours.

A red haze burned before his eyes and he cleared his throat to ease some constriction that had unexpectedly closed it off.

'Buenas noches,' he said hastily as Rose started at his approach, scrambling to her feet, her eyes wide as she turned towards him.

'How long have you been there?' Her tone was stiff with tension, warning him to stay away. A warning he had every intention of ignoring.

'Not long. But you seemed so absorbed, I didn't want to disturb you. '

He gestured with his hand towards the sketches that lay open on the table, a dress in a swirl of pink lace, the one she had been working on, uppermost.

'Aren't you supposed to hide those from me? Some ancient superstition about no one seeing The Dress until the big day.'

A wash of colour swept up into her cheeks at his teasing tone, and she moved the sketches around, fanning them out and then back again before answering him.

'Oh, no—that's just the bride's dress—Esmeralda's gown. And I'm past the point of drawing sketches for that. We've already had a couple of fittings and it's almost ready. These are some other designs—suggestions for the weddings of other clients. Women who were at the fashion show that night…'

She let the sentence trail away, but there was no mistaking which night she meant. Deliberately he waited and watched the struggle that went on behind her eyes before she opened her mouth again.

'I really am very grateful to you for what you did to help me.'

Grateful was fine. Even if she made it sound like something that was the exact opposite. He could use 'grateful'. He would have preferred something much more passionate, but at least it was better than the frozen mask that she slapped on her face whenever she was forced to be alone with him. She managed that as fast as she could, but he had still been able to catch the glint of awareness in her eyes, the way her white teeth had dug into the rosy softness of her bottom lip when she had thought he hadn't noticed her. But of course he'd noticed her. How could he do anything else?

His resolve to wait was coming back to bite him and bite him hard. Being with her and not being able to touch her in a sensual way was a torment, all the more so because it was self-inflicted.

He could sense where she was in the *castillo* even in the silence of the night, imagining her up in her suite, asleep on the high canopied bed or lingering in the deep roll-top bath, the water scented with some floral oil. Every instinct seemed to home in on her even when he tried to focus on something else. He could tell if she had been in a room and had left it just before he'd entered by the whisper of her soft slippers in a corridor, the trace of her perfume that drifted on the air. And to sit in a room with her, hear her voice, the bubble of laughter that seemed to well up so often when she was sharing something with Esmeralda, made his skin feel too tightly stretched across his body, pulling painfully taut across his scalp.

Just to watch her move across a room, see the sway of her breasts and hips, the smooth curve of her behind, the length of her legs, made his blood pound, his groin ache. This was why he had never been able to forget her. It was the reason for the burningly erotic dreams that had plagued his nights, forcing him to wake in a knot of sheets, with sweat sheening his skin. He had thought he'd suppressed those dreams after all this time, but from the moment she had come back into his life he'd been tormented all over again.

Being with her and not having her made him curse his blind stupidity in ever starting out on this idea. And now, when she had no trace of make-up on her porcelain skin, lush black lashes framing those mossy-green eyes, it was all he could do not to lean forward and crush the soft pink lips under his demanding mouth. Her long, fine hands were slightly stained with a wash of colour from the water-colours she was using on the designs, making a memory twist in his guts. Those fingers had once been smudged heavily with coal dust as she had tried to light a fire in the grate in their room in the squat, using a few battered, damp pieces of coal that had fallen from a passing delivery lorry in the week before Christmas.

'Perhaps I should save this for the big day itself,' she'd said, holding her grimy fingers out towards the weak, spluttering flame. 'Then we'd have something special to celebrate. But I can't wait…'

He hadn't encouraged her to wait either. Because it had been in that moment that he had resolved to make a move to change his life for her and with her. He'd known his father would demand a high price before he'd allow the prodigal son to return home, but it would be a price he was prepared to pay if it meant that he could offer Rose a better future. But he hadn't reckoned on her desertion, the betrayal that meant his Christmas Eve had begun with a visit from the police and had continued to go downhill from there.

It had almost lost him his honour, his family. And the damage it had done to Esmeralda was something he could hardly bear to remember even now.

'I've just been talking to my mother,' Rose said. 'I ring her every night and Maggie—the carer who is looking after her—has been a godsend. She and Mum are getting on so well, it's like having her best friend come to stay.'

He knew how that felt. When his father had been in his final illness, just four years before, the trained care of the professional nurses brought in to help him had been invaluable. He couldn't imagine having to cope with the round-the-clock care the old man had needed, and the business of dragging the estate into the twenty-first century without knowing that they were dealing with everything that was needed in his sickroom. They had also been able to keep an eye on Esmeralda too when he couldn't be there. But Rose had had to manage on her own. And her mother…

Her smile, the light in her face caught on a raw nerve. With the memory of that miserable winter day in the squat so clear in his mind, it was impossible not to contrast the way she looked now talking about her mother, and the bleakness that had dulled her hazel eyes when she had thought about not being able to be home at Christmas. *Infierno*, hadn't that given him the final push to hold out an olive branch to his father?

'I'm pleased for you.'

'For me?' She had obviously caught the distance in his voice and it made her frown. 'But you've been really kind to my mother and I'm glad to see her happy.'

'You can forgive her that easily?'

'Forgive—but she's my mother.'

'You ran away from her.' The memory made his voice hard.

'No!' Rose shook her head, sending her hair flying, the softness of it and scent of floral shampoo tormenting his senses. 'Not from her—from her husband.'

'She married him—her choice,' he dismissed. 'And she didn't protect you from him.'

'No,' Rose admitted with obvious reluctance. 'But she was scared.'

'And you weren't?'

'Nairo—I saw what he did to her. Her face—the bruises all over her body. Broken ribs.'

Her earnest tone, the expression on her face made it plain that it was important to her that he understood. And now, perhaps he did as he couldn't have done back then.

Her mother had been little or no help to her, he recalled, remembering the anger that had tightened his muscles, burned in his veins at the thought that in her own way Joy Brown had been as much of a waste of space as his own vindictive stepmother. That was why he'd been astounded to find that mother and daughter were now living together, with Rose doing everything she could to support her ailing mother. With a generosity he hadn't expected, she had obviously forgiven the older woman's neglect even before Joy had been taken ill. But then hadn't he been able to reconcile with his father once the old man, recognising how ill he was, had asked for his help after finally acknowledging the foolishness of believing Carmen's selfish lies?

I only wanted to give you and Meralda a new mamá... Raoul's voice, rough with the after-effects of too much wine, too many cigarettes, came down through the years

to haunt him. That would have been so much easier to believe if that 'new *mamá*' hadn't been an ex-showgirl who'd
worked in the casino where Raoul regularly lost more than
he could afford—and no more than six years older than
his adolescent son.

'Is it any wonder that I detest bullies?' he murmured,
seeing some of the tension leave her body as he spoke.
'In that case, I'm glad that I could help. So how is your
mother?'

'Making great progress. She's feeling stronger every
day and she sounds so relaxed. There's a new lightness in
her. It was like hearing her coming back to life. Really I
don't know how to thank you!'

'Ah, well, I can think of a way. I came to ask you something. Esmeralda has gone to spend the evening with her
fiancé and his parents, so I came to see if you wanted to
have dinner with me.'

'Oh—there's no need.' Rose placed her hands flat on
the top of the table in order to control the way that they
had started to shake nervously. 'I was looking forward to
a quiet night on my own. Perhaps a bowl of soup.'

'We can do better than that.' His smile burned through
the defences she had struggled to build around herself.
'I know that you've come here to work, but I'm no slave
driver. Surely you can give me a chance to say thank you.'

'Th-thank you?' Her tongue stuttered over the words
in the face of the unexpected warmth of that smile. 'No,
really, I am the one who should be thanking you.'

Nerves twisted into knots in her stomach, forcing her
to face the fact that she had no alternative but to agree to
his invitation. It would look so ungracious to refuse it now.

Besides, when he smiled like that, he made her forget
all about the man he had once been, the cold manipulator
who had been hidden behind the sexy, whipcord-lean youth

with unkempt black hair and gleaming eyes. But where had that youth gone—if in fact he had gone anywhere? Wasn't he just hidden under the sophisticated veneer that Nairo Moreno presented to the world? She had been deceived by him once and it had shattered her heart. Was she going to risk letting that happen to her all over again?

But it was only dinner, and here in this house. It wasn't even a *date*.

'It's only dinner,' Nairo said, echoing her thoughts with unnerving accuracy. 'Nothing to be scared of.'

'I'm not scared. Of anything.'

But it was too fierce, too emphatic to be fully convincing. As she watched that smile deepen in his eyes she suddenly knew that she was in big trouble. There was no way she could back out without making it obvious just what she had been dreading and so risking even further humiliation if she had this all wrong.

'Dinner, then.' She started packing away the sketches carefully in her portfolio. 'I hope you'll forgive me if I don't change my outfit. It's been a long day and…'

She let the sentence drift when he actually laughed at her concern.

'I'm only offering a casual meal, Rose. I'm not like my soon-to-be in-laws insisting on everyone dressing for dinner. I thought this would be an opportunity to escape all the formalities and relax.'

'Oh, that sounds great!'

Her relief was genuine. The past weeks had been something of a strain when she had found that she was expected to change for dinner every night. The formal meals around the highly polished table in the huge ornate dining room had been something of an endurance test and she'd already worn the few smarter dresses she'd brought with her at least twice. Her blue linen trousers and white sleeveless shirt were cool in the heat but hardly the sort of dressing up she had had to become used to.

'To be honest, I'm just in the mood for something simple like an omelette or cheese on toast.'

'Or fish and chips?' Nairo inserted lightly, taking the breath from her lungs with an instant vivid memory of just what had provoked that comment.

They had both managed to get temporary jobs in the run up to Christmas and to celebrate their first income in weeks had indulged in fish and chips, fresh from the paper, with fingers prickling from the icy cold. That cold now seemed to reach out from the past and encircle her heart. In spite of having so few comforts, and nowhere secure to live, she had thought that she was happier then than she'd ever been in her life before. Head over heels in love with the man she called Jett, she had adored and trusted him so much that she had given him her body, her virginity without fear or hesitation.

It had been less than twenty-four hours later when the bitter truth began to dawn on her as Nairo had started to talk about a way of making sure they had more money, a plan to secure their future.

'I don't eat chips any more,' she managed. 'Too much fat.' She regretted that comment as she saw the way it drew his burning gaze to her body, drifting slowly and deliberately over her shape, lingering blatantly at her waist and hips.

'You know you have no need to worry about that, Red,' he drawled, golden eyes challenging her to find an insult in his obvious admiration. 'And you don't have to fish for compliments.'

'I'm not fishing! And my name is Rose. No one ever calls me Red any more.'

'You'll always be Red to me.'

It was impossible to interpret just how he meant that comment and he didn't give her time to think about it as he turned to go back indoors.

'I can't offer you fish and chips, but I reckon I could rise to an omelette if that's really your choice.'

'*You* could…' Rose gave up on trying to hide her confusion as she was forced to trot in his wake.

That confusion grew even worse as she followed him, not towards the elegant dining room, where she had had all her meals so far, but across the tiled floor of the spacious hall and…out the main door?

'No—hang on a minute.' She hoped he'd believe her breathlessness was caused by her efforts to keep up with him. 'Where are we? I thought…'

'I invited you to dinner. You accepted.'

'Yes—but…' Unnerved, she looked back into the house, then turned again in time to see the amusement grow in his eyes.

'I thought you wanted a rest from the formality.'

'I did—but…'

'This way.'

He caught hold of her hand, leading her out into the still, soft warmth of the evening. Unable to break free without an awkward struggle, Rose let him take her with him along the gravel path towards another door set into the wall of the *castillo*.

'What is this?' she asked as he paused to slide a key into the lock.

'My home—my apartment.'

He flung the door open and stood back to let her past him.

'*Mi casa es su casa.*'

Rose stepped onto polished wooden floors, stared up at the high white-painted ceilings that soared above the hall-

way and the wide, curving staircase. Through the doorway
she could see a living room, with more wooden floors,
huge multicoloured rugs and large squashy sofas in a rich
deep red. The walls were lined with bookshelves and, even
at this point in the evening, the whole room was flooded
with light. As soon as she stepped into it, the room spoke
to her of comfort and relaxation more than any of the huge,
formal rooms in the main *castillo*. It had the same elegant
proportions of course as anywhere in the rest of the main
building, but it was so much more of a home than those
rooms with their old-fashioned, stiff furnishings.

This explained something that had puzzled her before.
She had assumed that Nairo had been out and about when
he didn't eat with his sister and her. That he had work to
do or he might have been wining and dining—and more—
one of the beautiful women he was so often seen with ac-
cording to the gossip magazines. She had never thought
that he might have this separate section of the *castillo* to
himself. Something about the room tugged on a memory
but one she couldn't bring to mind as it hovered on the
edge of her thoughts.

Nairo watched Rose stand in the centre of the room,
staring round at her surroundings, her confusion evident
on her face. He'd aimed for that and obviously he'd more
than succeeded. It gave him a grim sense of satisfaction
to see that this separate section of the *castillo*, his private
home, had surprised her as much as this.

It would surprise Esmeralda too if she had known that
he had brought Rose here tonight. He never brought anyone
to this apartment, least of all any woman he was seeing.
Those sorts of relationships were conducted away from
the *castillo*, in the woman's home, or the privacy of a suite
in a luxury hotel. The apartment was his, and only his. It
had been his refuge from the time he had come back from

Argentina, a place where he had the privacy and isolation that had never been his while his stepmother, or one of his father's more recent conquests, had been in residence in the main building.

His personal apartment had been a place of retreat when he returned to try to drag the value of the estate back from the brink of bankruptcy. A place that was his alone. Much as he loved his sister, and, towards the end, he'd rediscovered a connection with his father, he'd needed privacy for his own thoughts and a space to relax in.

Though relaxed was exactly the opposite of the way he felt right now. He didn't know what had possessed him to invite Rose here, to bring her into his private sanctum. He hadn't thought beyond the fact that he was tired of waiting, that he couldn't hold back any longer.

Seeing her in the main rooms of the *castillo*, with Esmeralda or perhaps Oscar and his family around, was becoming totally intolerable. He wanted Rose on her own. Just the two of them. The feelings she inspired in him were not for public times, for the company of anyone else. They were hot thoughts, burning desires that were just for the privacy of his own apartment. And ultimately for his bedroom.

But for now, he would play things casually; they had the whole night ahead of them.

'Pour yourself a glass of wine and come and talk to me while I cook.'

'You cook? You really meant it?'

'Of course—simple meals at least. An omelette, wasn't it?'

If he had offered anything else, she might have tensed up, decided this was a very bad idea, but this was so relaxed, so simple that it felt like coming home.

No! She couldn't let herself—wouldn't allow herself

to think like that. There was no way this apartment was anything like home to her even if the warm colours of the furnishings and the polished wooden floors were so very different from the formality of the main part of the main house, which had made her feel as if she were living in a museum most of the time.

'Pour one for me too.'

Nairo had headed through a door at the far side of the room, into the kitchen, Rose assumed. Spotting the bottle of rich red wine on the table, opened and left to breathe, she felt her heart hiccup once again.

Had he been so sure that she would join him? For a moment her steps turned towards the door, then she caught herself up, refusing to give in to the twist of nerves in her stomach.

She had told Nairo she wasn't afraid and she wasn't going to let him prove her wrong. Not when she had the chance of facing up to the mess their past had been and dealing with it once and for all. Determinedly she turned back, reached for the bottle of wine. She was lucky that she had already launched her steps towards the kitchen when the realisation of just why this apartment had seemed strangely familiar hit home with a head-spinning rush.

One night when the wind had rattled the window panes in the squat and they'd huddled together against the cold, she had spilled out some of her secrets, her fears, her unhappiness. Not just in her stepfather's home but before that, when her mother had struggled to find them anywhere to live, when one room had often been all they'd had to share together. Fred Brown's comfortable semi had seemed like heaven in contrast to that. At first. When they hadn't known the fear and distress that had hidden behind that safe suburban door.

In order to distract her, Nairo had set her to imagining what a real home would be like, creating the rooms in her imagination. Then he'd done the same. The place she was in now, she realised, was one of the rooms he had described to her then.

In the kitchen Nairo was already at work; he had pulled onions and peppers from the huge fridge and was busy slicing into them with a brutally sharp knife, his movements quick and efficient.

'Wine...'

It was all she could manage as she placed the glass beside him on the huge central island and then leaned back against the nearest worktop, sipping at her own wine as she did so. She couldn't take her eyes off his hands, lean and strong, and the speed and neatness with which he sliced and chopped. He had rolled the sleeves of his crisp white shirt back from his wrists to just above his elbows, exposing a long stretch of tanned olive skin liberally shadowed with crisp black hair. The way that the hard muscles bunched and moved under the satin skin transfixed her and she took another hasty swallow of the delicious wine.

Her whole body tingled under the memory of how it had felt to have those powerful, long-fingered hands stroke over her, making her quiver in uncontrolled delight.

'What is it, Rose?' Nairo had noticed her abstraction, and he paused in his preparations, dark head coming up, deep bronze eyes fixing on her face. He followed the track of her stare, glancing down at his arms, then flashing back up again to clash with her green ones. 'Not seeing what you wanted to see?'

There was danger in his question and in the darkness of the eyes that watched her intently.

'I—'

Straightening up, he stretched his arms out, flexing those elegant muscles all over again, as he waved his hands in her face. The burn from the acid onion juice on his skin made her eyes sting as she blinked in shock.

'No needle tracks, no scars, no trace of drug abuse. Not the arms of a junkie—hmm, *querida*?'

The hiss with which it was tossed in her direction made frightening nonsense of the term of affection so that her shocked and startled eyes lifted sharply, locked with his, unable to look away.

'Or do you think it all went up my nose?'

'No! Oh, no, no!'

She didn't even have time to rationalise her response, it was instinctive, escaping without a thought. Not this Nairo, the hard-working businessman, respected by so many, devoted to his sister...

But this Nairo was the same man as the Jett she'd known all those years ago. She'd been so *sure*.

No. It hit hard as a blow. She'd been so *scared*.

She'd thought she should fear him then, but the cold rage in his eyes told her that she had more reason to be afraid right now. And yet scared was not what she felt—not in the same way. Because she knew that right now that icy rage was justified.

'I never thought...I mean, I spent all those weeks with you. We lived together—I saw you night and day. Saw you dressed and...and...' her voice shuddered on the word '... undressed. I knew there was nothing like that. I knew that you were not an *addict*!'

She didn't know how she expected him to react. She only knew that it wasn't with the cynical laughter that made him throw back his head in a dark travesty of amusement. Disturbingly all she could think of was the way it had felt to lie in the sleeping bag with him, her head on his shoulder, nose pressed close against the bronzed skin of that strong neck, feeling the muscles move underneath it, breathing in the scent of his body. Even after ten years the memory still had an intensity that slashed at her heart.

'But you thought that I was prepared to feed others' addictions—for profit.'

If he'd raised his voice, shouted at her, then she knew she would have backed away, heading for the door. But his tone was flat and low, almost gentle, as if this were a casual conversation and not an exhumation of the darkness of the past that still lingered between them. Yet, for all that soft, steady tone, there was no hiding the ruthless control that went into keeping it that way. That had always been the difference between him and her heartless stepfather. But now she had to face the fear that that ruthlessness had blinded her to differences that went so much deeper.

She'd known this had to come sometime. At some point the silt that had gathered around their time together would have to be brought to the surface, exposed to the cold light of day. It was inevitable. But life had been so peaceful, so easy for the weeks she had been here that she had actually allowed herself to think that perhaps it didn't matter. That maybe she could complete her commission and get away again, unscathed…

Oh, who was she kidding? She hadn't been unscathed from the moment he had walked into her boutique and back into her life. The truth was that the past had left its scars, heart deep, and his return had shown that those wounds were still only barely healed. One word, one touch, one kiss like the one at the fashion show, and the delicate covering behind which she'd hidden them was ripped away, leaving her emotions raw and exposed.

The only surprising thing was that he'd waited so long. Why had he held back until now?

But then he said, 'And yet you were prepared to put up

with vile—my criminal past—in order to get this wedding dress commission?' And it all became so obvious.

It was for Esmeralda, of course. He'd wanted to make sure his sister got the dress of her dreams. Nothing was to come between that and the wedding. But now it seemed he was satisfied with how that had turned out and he'd decided to challenge her.

'You thought so little of me.'

She'd thought the world of him once and that was why disillusionment had hit so hard.

'I saw you.'

Nairo tossed the knife down onto the chopping board, clearly dismissing all idea of preparing any sort of meal for them.

'You saw what?'

'You—and Julie…'

'Julie?'

He could barely remember the name, but slowly the image came back to his mind. The bosomy blonde who had been the latest to warm Jason's sleeping bag, but who had made it more than plain she had an interest in him. Whenever Jason had been out of the squat she had tried to flirt with him, stroking his face, pressing unwanted kisses on his lips. But she'd usually waited until Rose was out too. Had Rose seen her…?

'Julie meant nothing to me.'

'Nothing?' Her wide eyes challenged that statement, but the sheen of tears that glistened in them told a different story. 'I saw you kissing her.'

'*Infierno*, you saw no such thing.'

Nairo reached for the knife again, pulling a pepper towards him and starting to slice into it, his movements hard and vicious. It was either that or reach for her—and he didn't know just *how* he would do that. Right now to touch her for any reason would blow this whole thing apart.

'You saw nothing. You saw *her* kissing *me*.'

'Oh, and you were fighting to get away from her, were you?'

Scorn and disbelief rang in Rose's voice and in that moment he knew just what kiss she had seen. The time when he had tried to convince Julie to get out of the squat—get away from Jason and his dirty deals. She had said that she would go if he went with her, her eyes even filling with tears when he had said no. He had tried to let her down gently, telling her that he was already committed. That had been the one and only time that he had admitted to anyone the way he had felt about Rose. He hadn't even told Red herself—something for which he was to be so very grateful later.

'No, I was not. But at least she didn't betray me.'

'Do you really think I could stand by and...?'

'And what, Red? And *what*?'

The knife slashed through the firm red skin of the pepper, hacking into the wood of the chopping board and leaving a cut so deep that he almost had to wrench it free.

'Fine—I kissed her—if that's the worst that you can accuse me of, then...'

Had she really just walked out on him because she had seen him comforting Julie? Had what they had meant so little to her that she could just turn her back and walk away? The slices of pepper dropped into rough, shapeless pieces, any attempt to dissect them carefully abandoned completely.

'So you didn't give her heroin?'

'What?'

Once more the point of the knife hit the chopping board and stuck, his fingers clenching so tight around the handle that his knuckles showed white. He couldn't make himself look at her, knowing that he would lose what little was left of his control if he did. Had she really thought him capable of that?

'You gave her drugs.'

His mind was back in the darkness of the squat, after that one lingering kiss. Lingering on Julie's part, never on his. He had tried one last time to make her stop, change the path she was on. A path that would lead all the way down to hell if she didn't get off it.

'Get out of here,' he'd told her. 'Get away and start again. That's what I'm going to do. I can't stay here any longer.'

He'd unpeeled her fingers from around the tiny wrap of drugs she'd clutched in her hand and held it up.

'No more, Julie,' he'd said. 'No more… If you leave it, you can come with me if you like.'

Was it possible? Could it be that Rose had actually seen that as him encouraging Julie in her habit, but, cold and controlling, he had told her she could have no more that day?

He knew—hell, he'd always known—that Rose had had good reason to go to the police. That the poisonous atmosphere in the squat had to be exposed and dealt with. Hadn't that been the reason he had wanted to get her out of there? The one thing that he had never ever been able to come to terms with was that she actually believed *he* was capable of being behind it all. So convinced that she hadn't even stopped to ask, to give him a chance to put his side of things. She had just turned and walked, leaving him behind without a backward glance.

Now it seemed that she had added other imaginary crimes to the list. But the ultimate betrayal was that, like his father, she had gone with what she had thought she'd seen, believing in the way things had looked rather than actually asking him for the truth.

'I gave her nothing.' The knife moved again, the sharp blade chopping faster and faster, dicing the pepper into tiny pieces. 'Not drugs. Not a thing.'

Absolutely nothing. Not a thing. How could he when at that time the only part of his heart that he had allowed to open was given to someone else entirely? To the woman who was standing at the other side of the island accusing him of...

His head came up, eyes blurred as he tried to focus on her face. The face that had once meant so much to him. Still so beautiful, but no longer the Red he had thought she was. The Red he had never ever really truly known. For such a short time she had made everything make sense— given him a path to follow, when all the while she had believed that he was lower than the grubby floorboards of the squat beneath her feet.

'Did you really think that *I* was the dealer in that place? That *I* was the one selling heroin?'

CHAPTER SIX

'TELL ME THE TRUTH. Is that what you thought?'

The expression on her face gave him his answer. But it was obvious that she couldn't hold back any longer.

'You had it in your hand that day and you suddenly had money. You said— You told me…'

I have a plan—a way of getting us out of here. The words hung between them in the stillness of the night, dark and determined and—as he now saw—so easily interpreted in a totally different way. By her at least. *But I need to get more cash together. Just give me a few more days.*

'I said I would get us out of there. I was working on it—but you didn't wait. You walked—you *ran*… You told the police that I…'

'I had to, Jett…'

Impossibly, she had reverted to the old familiar name, the one she had once used with warmth, he had believed, with love, he had deluded himself.

'I couldn't just sit back and let that happen.'

'Let what happen?' His voice sounded raw and cracked. 'Let *what* happen, Ms Cavalliero?'

'Jett—Toby *died* from an overdose, from a bad batch of that stuff. I couldn't let that happen again.'

'You couldn't— You— Oh, *infierno*!'

The curse broke from him as an unwary, unthinking

movement had lifted the knife again, bringing it down
onto one of his fingers, slicing in deeply.

'Hell…'

For a moment it was all he could say as the pain shook
him out of the daze of anger and denial that had held him.

'Oh, Nairo…'

Suddenly she was beside him, hands coming out, reaching for him. She took his fingers in hers, letting the knife
drop back onto the work surface with a clatter as she
turned towards the sink, taking him with her.

She turned on the taps, splashing water onto the cut
finger, letting it wash away the blood that had sprung to
the surface as she reached for a paper towel, folded it into
a pad and clamped it down onto the wicked-looking cut,
pressing it hard to stop the bleeding.

'Hold that—tight!' she said, her voice trying for author-
ity but threaded through with a quiver of concern. 'I'll find
something—do you have a first-aid box?'

'That cupboard over there.' He indicated with a nod of
his head. 'Second drawer.'

Rose found the sterile dressings easily, even though her
hands were shaking as she grabbed at them. Ripping off
the protective plastic, she was back at his side in a moment, seizing his injured hand with a roughness that betrayed the way she was feeling. The sight of the ugly cut
under the stained paper pad made her stomach roil and she
almost slapped the dressing down onto it, needing to hide
it. Stretching the fabric, she fastened it tight, then added
another one on top of it, making sure it was secure.

'Gracias.' It was raw, husky, and it made her keep her
head bent, her eyes fixed on his fingers.

The job was done; it was time to let go. And yet somehow she couldn't pull her hand away. Her fingers curled

around Nairo's, twisting, smoothing. She was stunned by how passively he let his own hand lie in her grasp.

'Thank you,' he said again, his voice deep and rough-edged in a new way that brought her gaze to his face. 'Rose…'

She felt she could drown in the fathomless pools that were his eyes. Her own face was reflected there, eyes wide, skin pale. Her hands still held, his but now it was for a very different reason. She felt the burn of his skin against hers like the sizzle of wild electricity, singeing her nerves.

'Rose, listen to me, damn you…'

His words seemed to scrape along her senses, making her breath catch and snag in her throat. She had to listen. She couldn't let go, couldn't move away.

'I did *not* sell any drugs to Julie or to anyone. You can believe me or not, but that is the truth. I was not dealing. I would rather die.'

He'd offered no proof, but the shock was that she didn't need any. The fact that he hadn't even tried to produce anything to convince her but had simply stated the facts hit her like a slap in the face, making her thoughts reel. How had she got it so wrong? How had she let herself be deceived so easily?

The full realisation came like a dagger out of the darkness, slashing at her in a way that wounded more brutally than the chopping knife had sliced into Nairo's finger. It had been there in the moment just now when she had realised how scared she had been when she'd been in the squat. Not just scared of Jett—but everyone. Anyone.

Her mother, her stepfather—they'd all let her down in their own way. Deep inside, wasn't the truth that she'd believed everyone would act that way? Particularly the men.

Even Nairo.

She'd thought she'd loved him, but had she truly trusted

him? Could you really say you loved someone without the deepest, most absolute trust?

The thought of the cruel wound she had just bandaged still made her shiver deep inside and now this new thought made the shudders colder, crueller. Had she let herself lose someone she had once cared for so deeply in the biggest mistake of her life?

Even as she asked herself the question there came a low, icy little thought at the back of her mind. Someone *she* had once cared for so deeply—but who had never actually said that he cared about her. She thought she'd loved him, but she hadn't trusted him to love her back.

'But the police...'

His grip on her hand tightened until she winced under the pressure.

'Oh, yeah, the police came—they had to, after you called them, didn't they?'

Molten bronze eyes burned down into hers, but Rose was back in the past, in the dark and the cold of that Christmas Eve. She had been unable to leave, to run as far and as fast as she should have done, and she had crept back to hide in the shadows across the street. She had seen the police raid the house, bringing out everyone inside. And she had seen Nairo bundled into a waiting car, speeding off towards the police station. Arrested, she had believed.

'No.' Nairo had seen the look on her face, watched the thought processes that changed her expression flit through her eyes. 'No, they didn't arrest me. Nothing to arrest me for. They searched the place, took everyone in for questioning—you should have stayed around longer. You might have learned a truth or two.'

That caught her on the raw, had her biting her lip hard, teeth digging deep into the softness of her flesh. There had been one moment when he had looked out from the back of the car, staring into the darkness. She had flinched back into the shadows, but…

'You saw…'

'I saw.' The confirmation was dark, brutally cold.

He'd seen her. He'd known she was the one who had reported him to the police. Who had had them raid the squat and arrest everyone they found there.

'I had to—surely you could see that? I couldn't have such a thing on my conscience…'

'And you thought that I had offended that delicate conscience? What was it, Rose—was it that, after your vile stepfather, you were seeing villains everywhere? So you thought I was one too? Or was it really something else?'

'What else could it be?' The way he'd come so close to her own disturbed thoughts earlier, the fear of what might be coming, made her voice tremble, her hands tighten on his.

'They found nothing on me, Red.'

Somehow he managed to imbue the once affectionate name with the burn of acid so that it seared over her skin, taking a much-needed protective layer along with it.

'Not a trace of powder, not a single syringe. There was nothing on *my* conscience, then or any other night. But there was plenty to find on Jason. It was Jason who was the dealer in that squat. So you see, you didn't earn your money—not really.'

'My money?' This was new, and unexpected. 'What money?'

She watched his beautiful mouth twist into a cynical sneer and in a sudden panic tried to pull her hands from his only to feel his fingers tighten around hers, holding her prisoner. She couldn't have moved away anyway. Her legs were numb, unfeeling as the shock of what he was saying punched into her chest, taking her breath from her.

'The reward that Toby's parents offered to anyone who could help them find who sold him the drugs that killed him. Wasn't that what stirred your *conscience* so that you just had to act?'

'No—no way!'

Once more she tried to wrench her hands from his, only to have those strong fingers curl around hers again, twisting so that he could pull her closer to him, her breasts crushed up against the hardness of his chest, his breath warm on her skin as he bent his head to stare straight into her eyes, searching deep as if to find the truth he wanted there.

'It wasn't— I couldn't...'

'Do you know, *querida*?' Nairo's drawl was slow and lazy, totally belying the intensity of his stare. 'If I wanted to, I could almost believe you.'

If I wanted to.

'But you don't—do you?' Rose snapped, fighting against the sharpness of the stab of that careless response. 'You want to believe that I only betrayed you to the police because it would profit me.'

His shrug was a masterpiece of indifference, brushing aside her protests effortlessly.

'It was a long time ago, a third of a lifetime—I've put it all behind me. And betrayed?' It came with a deadly softness. 'You might think that, my dear Red, but let me tell you that before I could feel betrayed, I'd have had to care.'

The poisonous bite of his words tore at her inside, though she was determined not to let it show. It was a fight to find more defiance against him, but she dragged it up from deep inside, tilted her chin higher, tightened her mouth.

'So you think that the only reason I could leave you was for money?' she flung at him. 'That otherwise you were so irresistible I wouldn't have been able to tear myself away? Did you ever consider that perhaps I'd realised that I wanted—*needed*—more?'

That memory slashed at her now, the one that had tormented her when she'd first come into this apartment and recognised it as the home that Nairo had described to her. He'd wanted her to respond with her own dream home, but she hadn't been able to do that. She'd had no idea what a real home looked like. Only that it was safe. With people she trusted.

'That I wanted what *Rose* wanted, what I have now— not to exist, as Red did, in a place like that, with a man like you?'

'If you did, then you were lying to yourself,' Nairo returned harshly, squashing her protest. 'And you've been lying for the past ten years with your Lord Andrew and your non-marriage.'

His dark head bent, came so close that his mouth was just inches away from hers. If she was to lift her head, then their lips would meet—and she shivered inside at the thought of the conflagration that would sweep through her if that happened. She feared it and yet she wanted it so much.

'You couldn't put anything in place of what we had— the passion that burned so hot and hard from the moment we met. That made me pick you up from the street where I found you. That made you give yourself—your virginity—to me without a second thought. You couldn't find anything to match it.'

There were no words to deny his accusation. She had wanted it then and, no matter how hard she tried to deny it now, she still felt exactly the same way.

No, not exactly. In the past she had fallen into his arms in the throes of her first, her only, blaze of naïve passion.

Nairo had come to her rescue when she had been lost and alone, homeless and helpless on the streets of London. She had thought that he was her knight in shining armour, her saviour. But he'd had nothing more than that passion to give her, and, needing so much more, she had let her fears grow until she'd convinced herself that she had no alternative but to run. But she'd been running from the lack of love, never from a man who dealt in drugs.

But the hellish thing was that even knowing that didn't change anything.

From the moment that she had seen the knife slice into his finger and had felt the shock of horror at the thought of his beautiful hand being damaged in that way, she had known she was in deeper than she dared to admit. Once long ago, in the squat, she had caught her hand on an exposed nail, just a graze, far less damaging than the knife cut, and instinctively he had reached for her, bringing her hand to his mouth, to kiss away the soreness of the shallow graze, looking straight into her eyes as he did so. She had loved the slow smile that had curved his lips, felt herself drawn irresistibly into the darkness of his eyes, and he had pulled her to him and crushed her mouth with his. They had ended up in bed—if the battered sleeping bag could be called a bed—that night, coming together again and again, only having to reluctantly put a check on the passion that burned between them when they had run out of the small supply of condoms that had been all Nairo could afford to buy.

She had been prepared to make love one more time without, she recalled, heat rushing over her body at the thought of how naïve she had been. She had never been able to impose any control on herself where he was concerned, as irresponsible as her mother, who'd been only the same age when she'd fallen pregnant. Nairo had always been the one to insist on a degree of sanity—out of consideration for her, she had always thought. She'd believed it was because he didn't want her to have to deal with unwanted consequences of their relationship so young. She had seen it as evidence of how much he cared, but later she had been forced to consider the possibility that it was really to protect himself. To ensure that he wouldn't be burdened with any responsibilities that might tie him to her for a future he had no desire to face.

Now she knew where he disappeared to at night, to this private apartment, she was again confronted with all the thoughts that had filled her mind when he hadn't joined them for meals, of Nairo being out on the town with a succession of beautiful women. In her imagination he had escorted them home, taken them to bed...

But perhaps if he had been here all the time... If he had spent the evenings in his apartment—alone?

Was she a fool to imagine that that was possible? To allow herself to think that Nairo had no one special in his life right now—no one, full stop?

The passion that burned so hot and hard from the moment we met. You couldn't find anything to match it.

Was it possible that that passion was the way he felt—had felt—still felt—too?

'You still can't, can you?'

'No?' She tried to make it into a challenge, bringing her chin up defiantly, but that only brought her lips even closer to his, the warmth of his breath on her skin, the taste of him so close that she could almost sense it on her tongue. 'You think not?'

She was teetering on the edge of a dangerous cliff, balanced so precariously that the tiniest puff of a breeze would send her flying, tumbling head over heels into the pit of molten need that was already threatening to enclose her.

She didn't want to say no, didn't want to put a stop to this. The need to acknowledge the reality of what he said was a burn in her veins, the tiny connection between their hands like putting her fingers into a live electric socket. She knew it was safer to let go—but at the same time she knew that it was the last thing she could do. She wanted this touch, needed more of it, as common sense fought a nasty little war with the hungry sexuality that was making her pulse thunder hard against her temples.

She wished he would make the first move, but deep down she knew that was just cowardice. She *wanted* this, she should own it, acknowledge it. If she chickened out now, she would only regret it so hard tomorrow.

But if she acted, would she regret it even more?

'I know not,' Nairo declared. 'If you'd found someone else to give you what we shared, then you would be with him now. But no, no one—definitely not your Lord Andrew. So can you face the truth—or can you actually claim that what I say is a lie?'

The danger was that he was talking to himself, Nairo knew. He wasn't just challenging Rose to admit how it had been, how it still was, for her, but forcing himself to look the truth in the face and review his own life in the ten years that had passed since they had been together. There had been no one else who had affected *him* so strongly, no other woman who had trapped him in her searing appeal, since the day Rose had walked out on him on that dark December night. Oh, there had been other women—too many—who had warmed his bed and eased the appetites of his body. But none of them had made him yearn as she had done. None of them had truly satisfied him.

They had been enough to stave off the hunger of his most basic needs, but he had left every bed with a feeling of emptiness and discontent so that in the end he had simply given up. He had nothing to give these women and they did nothing to fill the emptiness inside him. He had focussed instead on the work of the estate, the business deals that kept his mind from straying onto other, more sensual paths. In the beginning he had told himself that he was doing this only to rebuild his relationship with his father, to regain Raoul's respect, but the truth was that he was still trapped by the memory of how it had been with Red.

That was why he had had to keep her with him now. Why he couldn't let her go until he had gorged himself on her warm and willing body, to wipe away all the hunger she had left him with and know that at last he was done with the blind, foolish obsession he still had with her, sated and fulfilled so that he was at last ready to move on.

'No,' Rose said softly.

The single syllable was so unexpected that he felt it like a start inside his head, his gaze going to her face in shock, searching her eyes.

'Is that no, you don't want...?'

'No, I can't claim that what you say is a lie.'

If her voice had had the slightest shake in it, any sort of hesitancy, then he would have let her go, stepped away from her, forcing his attention back onto the preparation of the simple meal he'd been planning, though it would kill him to do so. He wanted her. *Infierno*, but he ached to possess her, to taste her mouth, feel the warmth of her skin under his touch, the softness of her body yielding to him.

But it was that *yielding* that he wanted. He wanted her willing and he wanted her as eager for his touch, his kiss, as she had been all those years before. Nothing else would give him the satisfaction he craved. He had been through every form of hell keeping his hands off Rose since she had come to live at the *castillo*, and now his blood was thundering in his veins so that he was hard and hot as hell, aching with need, unable to believe what she was saying.

'I'd like to be able to say that I don't feel that way about you, but I'd be lying...'

Nairo's only reaction was a long, slow blink, but she knew she'd stunned him.

'So?' Nairo questioned very softly. 'Rose, what are you saying?'

Could he bring his face, his mouth, any closer, without touching her? Did he know how much it tormented her to be this close and not to reach out to him? To be surrounded by the warmth of his body, the scent of his skin, feel his breath on her cheek? Her mouth had dried painfully and she had to slick her tongue over her parched lips in order to be able to speak. The way that his darkened eyes dropped to follow the betraying movement, the brush of the rich dark arcs of his lashes over the bronzed high cheekbones almost destroyed her.

'I—I...' she tried, failing to find any words to express the denial that self-preservation demanded she turned on him. The denial that would be every sort of a lie. 'I... Oh, Nairo...'

It could not be held back any longer.

'Kiss me! Kiss me now!'

CHAPTER SEVEN

Who moved first she had no idea. Had she lifted her face so that the tiny gap between their waiting lips was obliterated, bringing their mouths together in a clash of wild and searing passion? Or had he brought his lips down on hers in response to her wild-voiced demand? Or perhaps to silence any attempt she might make to deny what she'd said, to retract the command she had been unable to hold back?

He needn't have worried. There was no way that she could even consider denying the hunger that had been eating at her from the moment that he had walked into her boutique, back into her life. It was as if she had been asleep for the past ten years and like Sleeping Beauty had only been waiting for that one kiss from a very special prince.

A prince? Oh, who was she kidding? Certainly not herself. Nairo was no fairy-tale prince now just as he had never been that knight in shining armour she had dreamed of when she had first met him. He had promised her nothing, no happy-ever-after, but the truth was that now she didn't care.

All she wanted was Nairo the man, right here, right now. His brutally devastating kiss forcing her mouth open under his to taste the innermost essence of him, to let her tongue dance against his in intimate passion. The caress of his hard fingers on her skin, pushing under her blouse at the waist of her jeans, skating over her nerves so that she shivered in urgent response, pressing herself against the heat of his long body. Her breasts were crushed against the powerful wall of his ribcage, against her hips the hotly swollen arousal that told her he was feeling every bit of the hunger that seared its way through her.

In a burning haze of need, she felt her feet leave the floor as he lifted her, holding her in arms as strong as steel bands. With a moan of surrender against his demanding mouth, she flung her arms up around his neck, laced her fingers in the silk darkness of his hair and gave herself up to the feelings that were sweeping like a tidal wave through every inch of her.

'*This* could never be denied, never forgotten,' Nairo muttered against her lips, tugging at her blouse so roughly that buttons pulled off and fell to the floor with a soft rattle.

'Never…' she echoed him, unable to find any other words in the flames that took her mind out of reality and into a world where there were only the two of them and the heat that melted every barrier between them.

Her hands were shaking as they slid from his hair, tracing the powerful lines of his face, fingertips catching on the day's dark growth of stubble that shaded his chin. She couldn't believe that she had the freedom to touch him, to kiss him once again as she'd been able to do in the past. It seemed that if she opened her eyes she might find that the immaculate modern kitchen had disappeared and they had been transported back to the squat. Dusty and dull and cold it might have been, but to her it had been a special place. Because she had been there with Jett and because she had already lost her heart to him, all her illusions still in place, no thought of the way they were soon to be shattered.

'Never, never, never…' she whispered, cradling his chin in her hands so as to draw him closer, tracing the shape of his lips with her tongue so that she tasted his mouth, the faint salt of his skin.

But suddenly Nairo snatched his hands from under her blouse, bringing them out to close around her arms, as he lifted her from the worktop where she had been sitting, let her slide down the hot hard length of his body.

'No.'

It was rough and hard and unbelievable.

'No,' he said again. 'Not like this—not here...'

'Yes—here—now...'

Here, now, anywhere, any time. He surely couldn't be thinking of stopping.

But then to her relief Nairo moved again, swinging her up into his arms as he turned, taking her towards the door.

'I swore to myself that the next time I did this, I would have a bed to take you to,' he murmured into the fall of auburn hair. 'A proper bed—not some damn shabby sleeping bag on a cold hard floor.'

She had been perfectly content in a shabby sleeping bag on a cold hard floor, Rose told herself as he carried her across the room. Because then it had meant so much to her. She had been lost in the way she felt about this man; she'd never paused to have second thoughts about it. All her thoughts had been of him.

So when he laid her down on the softness of a wide, wide bed, the fine cotton smooth and cool under her heated body, she knew a tiny hiccup of hesitation, a needlepoint of doubt puncturing her need. It lasted all of the space of a couple of uneven heartbeats, only surviving until Nairo came down beside her, his hands caressing the need back into her body, his mouth exploring her face, her lips, the skin that those hands exposed as he pushed aside her blouse, unhooked the delicate lacy bra underneath.

Within moments Rose was adrift again, throwing her

head back so that he could kiss his way down the lines of her throat, across her shoulders. The warm, tantalising path his lips and tongue traced over the slopes of her breasts had her catching her breath in delight, arching her body up to meet his touch, increase the pressure of his kisses as the fire stoked up higher and higher inside her, throbbing at the hungry spot between her legs. When those tormenting lips curved over one pouting nipple, drawing it into his mouth where his teeth scraped gently over her skin before the swirl of his tongue soothed the faint sting in the same moment, it set up a whole new burn of need along every nerve.

'Nairo…'

His name was a choking sound of hunger as her hands held him closer, clutching at the powerful shoulders above her, and then, impatient at the unwanted barrier of his clothes, pushed their way between them to tug at the buttons on his shirt with as little care as he had shown hers earlier.

'I want…I *want*…'

'I know, *querida*…'

His voice had an edge of raw laughter at the urgency of her response, the words muffled against her skin as his wicked mouth teased her to even further heights of need, hunger burning out of control.

She didn't care that she showed it. Didn't mind what he thought when her own hands joined his at the waistband of her trousers as he eased the zip down, helping him to slide the garment down to her ankles, where she kicked it aside impatiently. She wanted to be naked with him, touched by him—oh, dear heaven, possessed by him! In her naïve foolishness she had lost all this ten years before and having rediscovered it now she could barely wait until Nairo made her his all over again.

Now she knew exactly why she had had to break off her engagement to Andrew. Why she had known all along that their marriage would have been the biggest mistake she had ever made. She had never felt like this, never known this all-consuming need with anyone but Nairo. And knowing that the mild affection she had only ever felt for anyone else, it was no wonder she had never been able to go through with taking their relationship any further.

'Red—Rose…*momento*.' The roughness of Nairo's voice betrayed the battle he was having with his self-control. Control that Rose didn't want him to hold on to.

'No…' She pouted her protests, her hands finding the buckle of his belt and flipping it open, sliding down the heated, swollen bulge of his erection, a smile curling her lips as she heard his groan of near surrender. But when she eased down his zip, sliding her cool hands into the heat underneath and feeling his long body buck in fierce response, she couldn't believe it when his hard fingers came down, closing over her wrist and holding her still.

'*Rose!*' It was a sound of reproach, the tightness of his jaw, his gritted teeth betraying the fight he was having with himself. 'We have to… We need…protection.'

Of course. If there was one thing Nairo had always considered whenever they had made love in the squat, it had been the need for protection. Somehow, in spite of the little money they had had, he had always made sure they had the condoms they needed, had never taken her to bed without them.

But there was something she needed him to know.

'Andrew…and I,' she managed as he levered himself up on one elbow, pulling out the drawer in the bedside table and reaching inside. 'I want you to know—we never…'

She couldn't complete the sentence. That tiny move

he'd made away from her let in a drift of air that cooled the mindless hunger just for a second.

But a moment later the heat and the need were there again as Nairo rolled back over her, covering her face with kisses that seemed even more ardent than before and that soon obliterated that moment of uncertainty. He tugged open the foil packet he'd grabbed, fingers uncharacteristically clumsy as he slanted his body away from her just for a moment.

'*Socorro.* Help me...'

It was a raw mutter of command, his hands reaching for hers as she aided him in sheathing the hardness of his erection, her fingers shaking as she felt his heat against her skin.

'Now...'

His impatience showing in the lack of finesse with which he pushed her back down onto the bed, Nairo's long body came over her, powerful, hair-roughened legs coming between hers, pushing them wide, coming so close to the hungry heart of her. Rose's eyes closed in anticipation, her head going back against the pillow, but even as she did so she heard his breath hiss in a sound of impatient dissatisfaction.

'No—*querida*—open your eyes. Look at me!'

His face was so close to hers when she obeyed him. His eyes glazed with passion, the high cheekbones streaked with red.

'I want you to remember this—to know who I am.'

'I know. And I remember...'

Her words broke off on a high wild cry of fulfilment as he thrust, hard and fierce, between her legs and up into the waiting, moist and yearning core of her body, making her close her hands over the powerful shoulders above her, her nails digging into the rigid muscles of his back.

When he began to move, she had no choice but to go with him. She rose to meet each thrust, sighed a release as he eased away, breath catching in her throat as she opened up more and more each time, giving everything she could, taking as much as she could get from him. It was hard and fast and ferocious as if the missing years had been stored up in the sexual hunger that now brought them both together in the wildness of their need. She welcomed the almost roughness of his passion, welcomed it and matched it as it took her higher and higher, pressure building and building until there was nothing left, nowhere to go but into the starburst eruption of total completion as they reached an explosive climax together.

Nairo woke early in the morning, as the dawn crept over the horizon and began to lighten the room, revealing the figure of the sleeping woman at his side, her auburn hair spread out across the pillow, her cheek cushioned on her hand.

His whole body ached in satisfaction in the same moment that just looking at her, at the soft swell of her breasts against the white linen of the sheets, the curve of her hips, the dark triangle of hair at the juncture of her thighs, sent a pulse thudding through him all over again. It roused a hunger that had been ten years building and from which nothing, not even the deep sleep of fulfilment that had finally swept over him, could distance him. He had Rose in his bed again after all this time and it had felt incredible.

It had been the best sex of his life, the sort of physical connection that he had been looking for all these years. It was what he had wanted ever since he had been with Red back in those days in the squat. Inexperienced as she had been then, she had been just a promise of what he now knew he had been searching for and why. Once he had found her again, he had had to keep her with him to anticipate just a moment such as this. To wake with her beside him, having taken her again and again until they had both tumbled into exhausted and satiated sleep.

At some point in the night, he had gone into the kitchen and fetched fruit and wine, a very belated replacement for the omelette that had never materialised. He had fed her grapes and peaches, licked the juice from her kiss-swollen lips. Then, when the shivering response of her body had made her spill some of the wine down onto her naked breasts he had lapped that up too, delighting in the way that her skin quivered under his tongue, the soft moan that escaped her mouth.

'So what happened to you after you left the squat,' he had asked at one point in the night when the darkness in the room hid their faces from each other, the expressions that might have betrayed more than their words could ever do. 'Where did you go? Surely not back to that bastard of a stepfather?'

He knew she'd reconciled with her mother, but surely she couldn't have gone back there. This time the shiver was far less sensual, far more a gesture of distress.

'Never! I couldn't have gone back there to save my life. But I got in touch with my mother—rang her when I knew he wouldn't be at home.' Her voice sounded bruised with the memories she was so reluctant to unearth. 'She was so unhappy—she realised just what this man she'd married was like and, like me, she was desperate to escape. We arranged to meet. But then she ended up in hospital.'

She paused, took a deep swallow of her wine as if finding strength to go on.

'She was bruised and battered. Broken ribs. We planned to get away together—leave him behind and make a new life for ourselves wherever we could. We had no money—

Mum wouldn't take anything from him and he'd controlled all the finances—but we didn't care. We contacted social services—they found a flat in another town, and we took whatever jobs we could find.'

Nairo levered himself up at her side, looking into her shadowed face. She had some courage, he had to give her that.

'And how did you end up with the designer's job?'

Rose tapped the edge of the glass against her teeth, gathering her thoughts.

'I found a job shelf-stacking in a supermarket—Mum and I worked in the same place. When I could, I started with evening classes—art and design—found I had a flair for that. When Mum found a better job I tried for college—won a scholarship. I worked in the evenings doing repairs and alterations at first, then I made a few dresses for people locally and I was lucky. People loved what I made. From that I got a place in a fashion house. I started at the very bottom, trained, worked hard…'

Her teeth flashed white in the shadows as she gave a slightly forced smile.

'I was lucky that I found some premises at an unbelievably low rent, and I seemed to get a reputation just by word of mouth. Then Mum found out she had cancer— and I met Andrew…and it all went downhill from there.'

'You never slept with him?'

He sounded as if he couldn't quite believe it.

'Never.' Suddenly she looked up at him, eyes shadowed in the moonlight. 'I never wanted to.'

Nairo's head went back sharply as he frowned his disbelief.

'But you wanted to marry him.'

'I said yes to his proposal.' Somehow she made it sound so very different from 'wanted to marry him'. 'I thought

Andrew offered me safety.' Her breath hiccupped on the word. 'But safety wasn't what I really wanted.'

It was supposed to reassure, but somehow it had a shockingly opposite effect.

'Safety,' Nairo repeated. 'As opposed to...'

Suddenly he slammed his wine glass down onto the cabinet at the side of the bed. Did she still think he was the dangerous one—the lawbreaker?

'If you wanted the bad boy...'

'Nairo, no! I had it all wrong. I was wrong. I should never...'

He couldn't stop himself from responding even though he knew his furious nod of his head had shocked her rigid.

'Yes, you should,' he growled. 'If you truly suspected that anyone—that I was involved with that filth, then of course you had to do something about it.'

'If I suspected...' She reached out, took hold of his hand as she leaned towards him. 'I did—but I was *wrong*. About you. And if you must know, I was wrong about Andrew as well.'

But that new mention of the man whose ring she'd worn was too much. He didn't want any thought of her past fiancé intruding into this night with her.

'Forget that man. He has no place here. All that matters is you and me.'

He'd taken the glass from her hand, placed it on the bedside table next to his own. Then he'd leaned over her, pressing his mouth against hers, kissing away the regretful words. As he'd known she would, Rose had returned his kisses, softly at first, then more hungrily, passionately, her mouth opening under his, her hands coming up to lace around his neck, pulling him down to her. She'd slid down on the pillows, taking him with her, the stroke of her hands turning from gentle to teasing to demanding in the space of a couple of heartbeats.

The next moment they had forgotten all about talking, or thinking, and had lost themselves in the wild, blazing passion that totally consumed them.

And now she was still here, beside him, naked and warm. All he had to do was to waken her...

But something stayed the hand he reached out to touch her, held it hovering over her body, so close that when she breathed in and out, slow and deep, the warm, flushed flesh of her breasts almost brushed against his palm.

If that happened, then he knew that so much else would happen too. He would not be able to control his response. Already his body was hardening in fierce anticipation of the pleasure it had known during the night and hungered to know again.

But know with *who*? Who was this Rose who had welcomed him into her warm and willing body so often in the night, and who lay there now, an open invitation to the heated oblivion he had known?

Was this the woman who had walked out on him without a backward glance, leaving him to face the police? They'd had nothing to convict him on, obviously, but the scandal of that raid on the squat and subsequent arrests had damn near destroyed every chance he had had of a reconciliation with his father.

Rose stirred, sighing softly, and Nairo pulled his hand back further, away from the temptation she offered.

Had she truly not known about the payment for information about the drugs that had taken Toby to his death? He had always believed that that had been her motivation for going to the police, and Jason, spitting fury at being found out, had vowed vengeance on her for exactly that.

Roughly he pushed himself up and out of the bed,

the jerky movement echoing the disturbed nature of his thoughts.

So what if Rose hadn't known about the reward? She'd claimed she loved him, but she hadn't trusted him. Like his father before her, she hadn't believed in him enough even to *ask* for the truth, going by what she'd seen, not by what she should have known of him. Then she'd seduced him into staying in the squat that night when he had planned to leave, to meet his father, to start the peace process that he had hoped might see him back in the family home.

But 'No—don't go...' Rose had pleaded, stroking his hair, his face, and pressing her gorgeous body softly against his, curling around him and doing that amazing little shimmy of her hips that had him hard and hungry in a moment, totally unable to resist her.

He was already burning erect now, just remembering it. So much so that it was uncomfortable and difficult to pull the zip of his jeans closed over his straining hardness. Every nerve in his body urged him to stop the crazy behaviour of pulling on his clothes—to throw them off and get back into that bed with Rose once again...

'Nairo...'

For a moment he wasn't sure if the soft voice he heard was in the past or behind him until the repetition of his name brought his head round to see where she had stirred in his bed, sleepy eyes only half open, a faint frown drawing her brows together.

'Where are you going?'

She levered herself up on the pillows, pale skin flushed from the warmth of the bed, the marks of his touch, the tumbled auburn hair falling over her face. Her mouth was still swollen from the passionate kisses he had pressed on her through the night.

'Don't...' was all she said and it was enough to stop him dead in his tracks.

'Come back here.' She held out a hand to him, regarding him through those half-closed eyes. 'Please.'

It was too much, and, with a groan of surrender that came close to a sound of despair, he tossed aside the tee shirt he had been about to pull on and threw himself down on the bed beside her. Gathering her slender naked body to him, he kissed her hard and let the waves of sensuality break over his head, taking him down, deep down under the surface until he was lost to the world.

CHAPTER EIGHT

It HAPPENED AS she left Nairo's apartment.

That last time had been so very special, their lovemaking holding such an intensity, a sultry passion such as she had never known. Nairo's kisses seemed to draw her soul from her body, his touch leaving a trail of fire wherever it had caressed her skin until once again they had both fallen into a deep pit of exhaustion from which Rose had only just managed to wake before it was too late. After snatching at her clothes and pulling them on hastily, she made for the door.

She thought that she had slipped from the bed quietly enough not to be noticed, her bare feet silent on the thickly carpeted floor, but it was as she reached the door that she heard Nairo stir in the bed behind her.

'What are you doing?'

His voice was muffled by the pillow, but there was no mistaking the sharpness of the question.

'I have to go! You know I do. If I stay, I might be seen by one of the staff, perhaps even Esmeralda. Or, worst of all, one of Oscar's family, particularly Grand Duchess Marguerite. She always wakes early. Do you want people to know about…us?'

Was there an 'us'? Or had their time together just been

a one-night thing? Never to be repeated? To be kept hidden like a dirty little secret.

If she'd done this before—all those years ago on the night when she'd crept away from him in the squat. If she'd stayed, curled back beside him—or just *asked* him what was going on—might she have discovered then how different things had been, rather than the way she'd believed them to be? If she'd asked him, would he have told her...?

'Jett...'

The old name was just a whisper, a sliver of sound barely escaping her lips, and she was convinced he hadn't heard it. She heard him shift in the bed, turning his face on the pillow so that he was looking straight at her.

'No—you're right.' It was curt, dismissive. 'That would be a bad mistake. You have to go...'

A heavily indrawn breath signalled a darker change of mood.

'And the name is *Nairo*,' he said with brutal emphasis. 'Jett never existed in the same way that Red was just a fantasy.'

'Of course...'

Now she really did have to go—and not just for fear that someone in the main house might see her. She had completely lost control of her emotions and the burn of despair inside her was something she would do anything to conceal from him.

She had thought that she'd learned from the past. That she should talk to Nairo, ask him what he felt, what was happening, rather than just running away. So she'd asked. And the answer he'd given had made it plain that there was nothing special between them. Only the wild, blazing passion that had raged through them last night and killed rational thought. The hunger of desire that needed no explanations, no feeling, no *caring*.

That was all that Nairo had to offer her, and if she was going to be strong enough to take what he had to offer for as long as he offered it and not ask for more, then she had to hold herself in and never let anything of the true way she was feeling show. If he had wanted more than they had already, then he would have made it plain. She didn't dare to push it any further.

To do so was to risk blowing even this 'relationship' wide open and destroying it completely.

'I'll see you back in the house...'

Where she would show him the calmest, most unemotional face he could want. If this was all he had to offer her, then she'd take that and not ask for more.

Somehow she made it down the stairs, gripping onto the bannister with tight fingers, blinking hard to drive the tears away.

But still they blurred her vision, blending with the hazy light of the dawn to create a cloudiness that meant she could barely see as she made her way onto the path around to the main door of the *castillo*. So when a sudden bright, vivid flash came out of nowhere, blinding her, she thought it was more of the same distortion of her vision that resulted from the stinging moisture in her eyes.

Until it came again. And again, suddenly becoming a fusillade of sparks and flares blazing out around her into the silence of the morning.

It might have been ten years before, Nairo told himself as he watched the door settle back into its frame behind her. With Rose creeping from his bed to leave him without a word. Except that then he had barely stirred as she had slipped away from his side. He had never even suspected that she had gone for good.

Would she be back this time? Did he want her to stay?

Hell, he wasn't finished with her yet, that much was sure. The side of the bed where she had lain was cooling rapidly, but that wasn't the only reason why that space felt empty. He didn't want this night to end, didn't want Rose to leave. And not because he was concerned that the Schlieburgs would see her, though that seemed to be what disturbed Rose—what she seemed to expect that he would be troubled by.

Oh, he was quite sure that Marguerite wouldn't be too happy to find that he was sleeping with the hired help! But she would come round to it. Unless of course it affected the preparations for the wedding if the news got out, which, with what he'd seen of the reactions to Rose's past, it well might.

It was obvious that Rose wanted to keep it hidden, and expected that he'd feel the same way. He'd let her think that. Because the truth was that he wasn't ready to share this change in their relationship with the world. He knew that she believed that was because of a concern for the in-laws. That the prim and proper Schlieburgs were always in his mind whenever he acted right now. But the real truth was that it was less Esmeralda's new family that concerned him, but his sister herself. If he came out into the open about that fact that Rose was his mistress, then Esmeralda would read so much more into it. She would look into his face and see things that he didn't want her to see.

Or was there something more to it than that? The uncomfortable twist in his guts had him sitting up sharply, staring into the mirror on the wall, meeting his own eyes, searching to see just what was in the face he presented to the world now. He knew what had been there ten years before. The anger, the sense of betrayal, the loss.

Don't be long, he'd said and she'd promised him that she wouldn't be. But then she was gone and that was the last time he had seen her for ten years. Ten long, hollow years, he admitted now, acknowledging deep inside the emptiness he'd endured when she'd left him. He had been so sure that everything was going to be right. She had reached for him, had loved him—or so he'd believed—opening to him so warmly, so willingly, so generously, so heartfully.

But the truth was that she had used his desire for her to keep him right there in the squat until it was too late for anything else, until she had known that the police must have been on their way, and then she'd tossed that cool 'I won't be a minute...' at him and walked out of his life.

Or had she? Raking both hands through his hair, he forced himself to face the new thoughts that had intruded into his mind as he had come awake. There had been a difference, something close to desperation, in the way she had reached for him that long-ago night. Something that, recalling it now, had jarred so badly that he had reacted angrily when she had called him Jett. It had not been a comfortable experience being reminded of the man he had been then.

He'd still been smarting from his father's brutal dismissal of him, the way he'd been thrown out of the family home on the word of his lying stepmother. His judgement had been way off. He'd seen Rose as just another deceitful female who'd come between him and his family, ruining his good name all over again in his parent's eyes. That had been the final slash of the emotional knife that she had used to cut away every last trace of the connection they had shared, destroying the chance he'd thought he'd had of taking it further, making it work.

But he hadn't shared his plans with her. If he had asked her to stay that Christmas, told her about his plans to reconcile with his father, what would she have done?

He pushed himself upwards, throwing back the sheets as he reached for his jeans, pulled them on, dragging a

black tee shirt over his head. This time there had been
something else in her voice. A muffled, thickened sound
that had made it seem as if she was upset.

Was it possible that there was more to it than he had
suspected? he asked himself as he dashed down the stairs,
out the door. Perhaps if he caught her up, made her talk to
him… Perhaps there was something they could salvage…

He came to a violent, abrupt halt, the shaken, devas-
tated realisation of just what was happening stopping him
dead as he saw Rose some way off across the lawn…and
the sudden frenzy of brilliant camera flashes filling the
silence of the morning.

'Señorita Cavalliero…'

'Miss Cavalliero… Rose…'

The chorus of voices, some English, some speaking in
Spanish, came at Rose out of the half-darkness, all firing
questions at her. All the time the barrage of camera flashes
went off right in her eyes until she threw up her hands to
shield her face from their glare.

'Hey, come on, Rosie, give us a smile! Talk to us!'

'What do you want?'

She'd been through something like this when she'd broken off her engagement to Andrew, and that she'd understood. She'd left things to the very last minute and the
plans for the wedding had been in the public eye for a few
weeks. So she'd felt she deserved it when the paparazzi
had descended on her shop, firing cameras in her direction, hurling questions she couldn't answer.

But now…

'When did this all start up, then, Rose? Been going on
long?'

'How does it feel to be another notch on Nairo Moreno's bedpost—or is he a notch on yours? Is this why you
dumped Andrew?'

'Will you be showing Señorita Moreno how to run out on her wedding at the last minute as you did?'

'No! Nothing like that!'

Rose kept her hands in front of her face as she tried to move forward, struggling to see her way along the uneven path. The reporters and cameramen were closing in on her on all sides, pushing and shoving, setting her off balance so that she stumbled awkwardly.

And would have fallen if strong arms hadn't suddenly come out to grab hold of her, haul her upright again and hold her tight against something warm and hard and supportive.

Nairo. Nairo's hands holding her. His arms keeping her upright, his powerful chest and long body providing the support she needed to stay on her feet. The heat and scent of his skin surrounded her and made her feel warm and safe, enclosed in a protective shell. She heard the buzz of excitement from the pestering reporters but couldn't bring herself to respond to it.

Luckily she didn't have to. She felt Nairo draw in a deep breath, then heard his voice, calm and strong, coming over her head to reach her tormentors.

'Gentlemen…'

She could hear the irony in his tone, feel the fight he was having with his own forceful nature to keep the control he clearly believed was necessary.

'Stop harassing my fiancée.'

No, she had to have heard that wrong, He couldn't have said… But even as the sense of shock reverberated through her she saw the same effect hit the reporters as they stilled, silenced, stared.

'I—' she tried, only to have Nairo squeeze hard where he held her. Then he bent his head to brush his lips against the side of her face.

'Let me get rid of them.' It was soft enough to be inaudible, especially when another thunderstorm of camera clicks and flashes drowned every other sound.

'Nairo…' Rose tried to protest, but he silenced her with another kiss, longer and more lingering this time, right on the lips she had parted to protest, creating a new frenzy of interest and making her mind whirl in confusion. Then he spoke over her head as he addressed the paparazzi.

Yes, the engagement was a recent thing—very recent. But not unexpected. Nairo had fallen for Rose from the moment he saw her, but he'd wanted to wait so as not to interrupt his sister's wedding and take the attention away from the bride-to-be. No, they hadn't even chosen a ring yet, though, in his family, tradition usually decided on that.

Rose heard his answers through what sounded like a thousand bees buzzing inside her head. The shock of the ambush by the reporters, the unexpectedness of Nairo's arrival, the solution he had adopted to explain their situation and that kiss had all combined to scramble her thoughts so completely that she couldn't be sure she was hearing anything right. The one thing she was sure of was that the reporters seemed happy with the story they'd been given. If she interfered now, contradicted anything Nairo said, then it would only make things so much worse.

So she managed to stand at Nairo's side, his arm around her waist, her body pressed close to his, and watch and listen as he appeased the scandal hunters by giving them what they obviously thought was a story worth a banner headline and a couple of the photographs they were still busy snapping as fast as they could.

'Spanish aristocrat to marry designer who ran out on her own wedding!' She could imagine the headlines now, and that made it a struggle to obey the hissed command

of 'Smile!' that Nairo gave her with a swift tightening of the arm that held her.

She knew what he was doing and why he was doing it even if the reporters didn't suspect. She recognised the defensive mode that Nairo had slipped into from the moment he had caught up with them and found her hounded by the pack of reporters. He was making the best of a bad job, putting a new spin on the fact that she had been caught sneaking from his apartment after what had obviously been a long night spent there with him. The very last thing that he would have wanted to happen before Esmeralda was married to her duke. This was his personal nightmare come true—the one he'd warned her he would be furious if it materialised. He was making sure that at least when his sister's soon-to-be in-laws heard about this—as now inevitably they must—they would not be appalled at the thought of a raging sexual affair but hopefully more tolerant of a couple who were secretly engaged but had held back from announcing it in consideration of the fast-approaching wedding.

'Gracias, señores...'

Nairo had obviously defused the problem for now because the reporters were packing up equipment, turning away, the story ready for filing for tomorrow's news.

Clearly Nairo thought so too because he grabbed hold of Rose's hand and almost dragged her in the direction of the main house. Yanking open the huge carved wooden doors, he pulled her into the tiled hallway and leaned back against the wall, letting his breath escape in a hiss of forceful relief blending with a sound of barely repressed fury.

'Hopefully that will hold them,' he muttered, releasing her at last.

'Hold them!' Rose spluttered, not knowing how to express the mixture of feelings that were curdling inside her. 'How can it hold them when you've just delivered a story that will run and run? They'll want more and more of this fiction...'

'I only said that we were engaged.'

Nairo looked down at her with an expression that made her wonder if she had suddenly grown an extra head. No wonder when the emotional battle going on inside her had made her voice tight and constricted like the control she was struggling to impose on the sudden rush of sadness that had swamped her at that 'I only said...'

Only. There was nothing only about this where she was concerned. The casual way that Nairo had dismissed the idea of an engagement between them—even a pretend one—as having any importance made it only too clear the size of the chasm between them on this.

It meant nothing to him but a pragmatic way of dealing with an unexpected problem and it didn't matter who else was involved or whether they agreed to his approach or not. While for her, the word *engaged* burned like a branding iron.

Add to that the fact that Nairo had only decided to bring their relationship out into the open because it had been forced on him. He'd used this way of explaining it because of the impact it might have on his beloved little sister. Rose might find herself on the pages of the gossip columns, Nairo might now have to tell his family about their relationship, but the truth was that she was really nothing more than his dark little secret, something he would have preferred never to let anyone know about.

'But *engaged*!' Rose echoed. 'Why did you have to say that?'

'It's the only thing the Schlieburg family will understand,' Nairo returned, his expression making it clear that she should have known that. 'If we are planning on getting married, they'll accept that. But a casual hook-up...'

His mouth twisted wryly and he shook his head.

'Not so good.'

'And what when this thing is over and we go our separate ways?' There was an awkward crack of her voice on the words.

A shrug of his powerful shoulders dismissed her question carelessly.

'Engagements break up.'

'But it will be too...complicated.'

It was the only word she could find. *Complicated* came nowhere near what she really meant. She had broken away from this man once before and it had been hell living with the memories. Those memories had even pushed her into the total mistake of her relationship with Andrew and got her the reputation as a heartbreaker when the truth was that it was her own heart that had been breaking at the thought that she seemed incapable of loving anyone else after losing Nairo.

So what did that mean for the way she felt about him now? She had ached with the loss of him even when she had believed that he was the drug dealer she had felt morally obliged to hand over to the police. Now that she knew more about that situation, recognising deep in her soul that she had made a bigger mistake in even suspecting him than giving him her heart, how did she feel about the man himself? She wanted him like hell, that much was obvious, but more than that?

Oh, it was pointless even questioning herself about it. He had made it plain that she was nothing more than a sexual fling for him. This affair was the leftover embers of the carnal passion that had flamed between them so powerfully all those years ago. They had never had a chance to allow that fire to burn itself out, and the bonds of passion that had tied them together had only frayed, not actually been broken. They were still there, still tangling round them, refusing to set them free until they allowed this hunger to burn itself out. The young, foolish adolescent love she'd once known for Nairo had never vanished. Now it had grown into a powerful full-blown adult passion. The love of a woman for a man.

But was Nairo only set on indulging the physical hunger he felt for her until at last, sooner or later, he was sated and could turn and walk away?

The cruel ache deep inside told Rose that she strongly suspected that would be sooner rather than later. He had only actually acknowledged her this morning because the paparazzi had forced his hand. Left to himself, wasn't it more likely he would have kept her hidden away?

'Complicated is not really what you mean,' he said now.

'Of course it is.'

Nairo shook his head, golden eyes locking with hers.

'I told you that you couldn't lie to save your life.'

Which lie did he mean? It caught on raw nerves that he might have guessed something of her feelings, reading too much from her face.

'You're afraid that when we split up they'll think you've done it again—run out on your husband-to-be so close to the wedding day.'

Rose hadn't been aware of holding her breath tight in her lungs, but the sudden inward rush of air snatched in a moment of release made her head swim.

'You're right. That's it.'

She grabbed at the chance to hide the whole truth. Surely there was enough of it in that to convince him on this at least.

Shockingly gently, Nairo reached out a hand, traced a

single fingertip down the side of her face until it came to rest along her jawbone. This time he actually did let the control over his expression melt into a sort of a smile.

'Don't worry, *querida*—I'll take the blame. When the time comes, I'll give you plenty of cause to break it off. Everyone knows I'm not the marrying kind, and you're unlikely to change that. All you'll have to do is to look like the broken-hearted fiancée. Everyone will be on your side in this.'

Even you. Rose dropped her eyes to the floor for fear he might see something she wanted to hide. So now he would be considerate when his thoughts were all of breaking up with her. Did he have to make it so blatantly clear that he just wanted to get her out of his system?

But then she should have expected this, shouldn't she? This was the same man who all those years ago had sent her running with his cold-blooded declaration of *I don't do love. I don't do commitment...I certainly don't do marriage.* And now he'd just reinforced that statement every bit as strongly, if perhaps a little less harshly.

Nairo Moreno or Jett, it didn't matter which incarnation of this man she was with, he'd stated openly that commitment was not in his vocabulary. While she seemed to fall in deeper with every breath she took.

'Great.'

She could have tried harder to make it sound convincing, Nairo told himself, but she hadn't even bothered to inject a note of resolution into her response. He had offered her a way out of the mess in which they'd suddenly found themselves, but she didn't appear to give a damn about it.

He'd come hurrying after her, wanting to talk. Willing to admit that the past had been full of mistakes, marked by emotional scars they'd both carried. That perhaps the present could be different. That had all been shattered in

the moment he had seen her beset by the gang of reporters. He hadn't paused to think. Had only known that he
couldn't let her be exposed to the scorn and ridicule that
had been directed at her before by Geraldine and her type.

'Well, at least we won't have to get divorced or anything
messy like that,' Rose said carelessly. 'That would really
upset your prospective in-laws.'

The flippant response set his teeth on edge; the muscles
in his jaw tightened so hard they actually ached.

'That is not going to happen.'

Things weren't going any further; he would just settle
for what they had. Like a fool he'd tried to push things ten
years ago, wanting to hold on to everything he thought he
could have. So he'd rushed into telling his father that his
life had moved onto a very different path. That he'd found
the woman who would make him change. He'd wanted
to show Raoul that he could settle down, become part of
the family again, and he'd thought that Rose would come
with him. But he'd moved too fast, assumed too much.
He'd learned the hard way how wrong those assumptions
had been.

Not this time.

'Our relationship is to be a tragic mistake. One we
rushed into but then realised we couldn't live with. If the
family ever think it was anything else…'

She actually recoiled from the intensity in his voice, her
mossy-green eyes opening wide to reveal the dark shadows swirling inside them. She had looked like that once
before. In the squat when he had told her that he had a way
of getting them out of there, with money to support them
both. At the time he hadn't realised that, believing so ill
of him, she'd been horrified at the thought of any sort of
future together. Just as now she couldn't make it plainer
that all she wanted was a sexual fling. Time to—what was

it she had said?—get this thing out of her system. *This thing!* Little Red had grown up—she had no fear of saying exactly how she felt.

'You're really over the top about looking after Esmeralda, aren't you? What created this obsession?'

She was getting uncomfortably close to memories he didn't want to probe.

'Is it an obsession to want your sister to be happy and cared for?' he growled. 'Surely that's a normal brotherly feeling.'

'Happy, maybe,' Rose acknowledged. 'But you seem prepared to do anything for her.' Even tie himself into a fake relationship he didn't want so that her in-laws would be happy. 'Don't you think it's OTT?'

Something flared in those amber eyes. Anger? Rejection? Or something else?

'She was only a kid when I left home—and she needed me. When I went back—when my father finally let me in—I promised myself I'd never let her down again.'

'Let her down?'

She'd seen the way he looked at his young sister—and, more importantly, the way that Esmeralda looked at him. Those weren't the looks between someone who had been let down and the person who'd upset her badly. The truth was that Rose had envied Esmeralda's close connection with her brother, the obvious complete trust she had in him.

'How did you do that?'

But that was obviously a question too far. His jaw set tighter, his face seeming carved from granite. Hardly surprising when she had touched on that all-important word *trust*. The one thing he had wanted from her—and the way she had failed him. The bitter twist of her conscience was nasty and sharp, making her suddenly need to sidestep this particular subject.

'So what do you mean, when your father let you back in? I was the one who had to get away—escape from having anything to do with my stepfather. So I couldn't risk going back home. You told me you were the one who just walked out. So, presumably you could walk back in?'

No response. Not a word or a change in his set, taut features. Suddenly she wanted to provoke him. Wanted the truth from him.

'It was OK for you, surely. You had a comfortable home, a business, family wealth just there for you.'

'Walk back in! Hah!' His tone was so cynical it could have flayed a layer of her skin away. 'You have to be joking.'

'Why? Wasn't it like that?'

'In my dreams. How could it be with—'

'With what?' Rose questioned when he broke off, turning his head sharply to stare out across the garden, where the sun was now beginning to burn through the dawn mist, refusing to meet her eyes. 'What happened? Nairo—tell me.'

CHAPTER NINE

'NOTHING TO TELL.'

The face he turned back to her was bleak and so ruth-lessly controlled that it seemed as if his cheekbones might slice through the skin where it was pulled taut and white against them.

'It no longer matters. It's done with.' He bit the words off with a brutal snap. 'In the past.'

If he expected her to believe that, then he needed to be more convincing. All that his expression conveyed right now was the fact that he was cutting himself off from whatever had happened, and his body was so rigid that it made her want to ease some of the tension away from his muscles.

'It might be in the past, but it's pretty obviously not done with. Not when it makes you look like this.'

With careful fingers she traced the drawn shape of his cheeks and jaw, feeling the muscles bunch under her touch. She wanted to soften it even more, perhaps risk a kiss, but she didn't dare. Every instinct told her that if she pressed her lips to his, then he would respond with that searing hunger that flared between them so fast. Light the blue touch paper and stand well back.

Even if she welcomed the thought of being taken to his bed again, of giving herself up to the passion that stormed her body, sent her brain spinning, she knew that if she did so, if she let him take her out of the here and now and throw her into the wildness of pleasure he could give her, then he would never let her go this way again. He would snatch at the opportunity to distract her totally, and so never tell her the truth, never let her into this particular dark space inside his mind.

'Tell me,' she urged softly.

'I told you. Back then.'

'Oh, come on!' Rose mocked. 'You told me only as much as you wanted me to know. Why do you think…?'

But that was treading on dangerous ground, going back to the confrontation they'd had the previous night. She hadn't trusted him. She'd been a naïve fool to think she could say she loved him when she had never really known him. But the man she was getting to know now, the man who cared for his sister, had worked so hard to regain his father's respect… Who, face it, had come to her rescue just now even if he had used his own pragmatic way of dealing with things, and so had trapped them both in a situation that he must hate. One that tore at her heart for the lie that it was.

'You told me that you had a row with your father and walked out.'

He'd made so little of it then that she had believed it had been nothing like the fear she had fled from in her own home. It seemed that in that, as well, she'd been badly mistaken.

'He threw me out.'

Suddenly he flung up his hands in a gesture of surrender and it was as if she had pressed the right button, and the stream of words couldn't be held back.

'My parents' marriage was toxic. She married him for his money and thought her duty done when she provided one heir—me. Two children were not in the contract, so she didn't stay around after Esmeralda was born.'

'She left when you were—what—nine?'

The sharp nod of his dark head held all the anger he wasn't prepared to express.

And his sister just a baby. It was no wonder that he had always felt so protective to Esmeralda as her big brother.

'We had nannies of course—and my father had plenty of women, but none of them stayed around very long. They just helped him spend his money and then moved on. But later *Papá* married again. My stepmother—my *much* younger stepmother—tried to seduce me. She came on to me one night, hot and heavy. I'd had a drink and, stupidly, didn't quite realise just what she was up to. But then when we were found in a compromising situation— she had half her clothes off and was starting on mine—she claimed I'd been the one who had started it all. My father told me to get out.'

The stark control was back, giving away only the most basic of facts. That in itself told Rose more than she wanted to know about what had actually happened.

'He cut off my allowance, threatened to disinherit me totally, said he never wanted to see me again. I can't say I wanted to see him either if he believed her word against mine.'

Rose flinched away from the flat coldness of that statement, knowing how much lay behind it. No wonder he had been so darkly angry at the way she hadn't trusted him either. With his father's betrayal behind him—both his parents' really—he would find that so very hard to forgive.

She wanted to reach for him again, bridge the gap between them with a touch, but even though they were barely inches apart the emotional chasm seemed too great to overcome.

'So I came to London, ended up in the squat.'

The look he turned on her actually had a glint of dark humour in it, an unbelievable smile tugging at his mouth.

'It wasn't just any old squat—it was actually once my family's London house. One my father had let become so run-down because he'd been spending all his money on women. To tell you the truth I quite enjoyed the thought of squatting in the family home. After all, *Papá* had left it to go to rack and ruin. At first it gave me some satisfaction to know my father would hate my being there—but later I had a crazy idea of standing guard over the property, making sure it wasn't totally destroyed by the others.'

His bark of laughter was cold and brutal so that she winced inside just to hear it.

'I should have realised then how bad things had got— how fast my father had gone through his fortune—and that was before Carmen divorced him and took half of what was left. But then, that Christmas, I decided it was time to try to build bridges. I contacted my father—offered an olive branch. He was hard work—I almost didn't make it.'

Another shrug of those powerful shoulders, another controlled, obvious understatement, hiding so much more. And her behaviour must have made it so much worse. She didn't need to be told; she could fill in the blanks for herself. His father had heard about the drugs bust and the police raid. He'd also learned that someone had died and had blamed Nairo for that.

'I'm sorry.' What else could she say? 'So sorry.'

His eyes were dark, shuttered as he looked down at her, but astonishingly he shook his head in rejection of her apology.

'What else were you supposed to do if you wanted to stop that awful trade that Jason was involved in? It was what I was going to do as soon as I got you out of there.'

For a moment she'd been so rocked by that 'what else were you supposed to do?' that she almost missed the final throwaway sentence. But even as she registered it, he was speaking again and that dreadful, flat, controlled tone allowed for no interruptions.

'When I was allowed back home, I found that the stepmother had left. She'd abandoned Esmeralda—who was only nine. That was the second time she'd lost a mother.'

Bitterness twisted the word into an appalling sound.

'The woman who gave birth to us walked out when she was only a baby. Now this one. And my father was busy with a new woman. I promised myself I'd take care of Esmeralda, but he said he wouldn't have me in the house unless I went to work on the *estancia* in Argentina—to "earn my place in the family".'

'Esmeralda told me you revived the *estancia*. You proved yourself with a vengeance.'

Nairo nodded sombrely.

'What did you do there?'

For the first time his face lightened. There was even a curve to his lips, a light in his eyes.

'I turned the place into a profitable venture by making it a popular holiday destination—horse riding, wine tasting. I even set up an arts trail—there are some brilliant new painters out there. My father must have hated the way it had become so commercial—but he couldn't deny how it started paying its own way. Especially when it ended up out of the red and completely into profit.'

'He'd have had to admit you did the right thing. And he must have let you come back home.'

'Yeah—but when I did Esmeralda had changed out of all recognition. She'd felt so out of control for too long. There was nothing she could do about the family situation, so she started to impose a ruthless control on something she could govern—herself.'

'I wondered if she'd had an eating disorder,' Rose put in on a gasp of shock. 'Was she anorexic?'

It was obvious when she thought about it. Esmeralda was so delicate, so bird-like. She almost looked as if a touch would snap her in two. And if this was what she was like now, some time since the events Nairo was describing, then what must it have been like back then?

'She almost died.' Again, the flat, toneless voice expressed the horror of that time.

'I understand,' Rose said, knowing she meant more than his sister's story. It was no wonder he was now so totally focussed on propriety and the family's reputation. That he wanted Esmeralda to be happy.

But he had lost his mother too. When she'd walked out she'd left both of her children, and Nairo, at nine, had to have been more aware of her abandonment than his baby sister.

No wonder he'd reacted with such ferocity when she'd told him her story, declaring that her mother should have been there for her, to defend her. That she hadn't deserved the—in *his* mind—too easy forgiveness Rose had given her. But for Esmeralda's sake *he* had been prepared to hold out an olive branch to his father, to work his 'penance' in Argentina.

And not just for his sister, a sad little voice in her thoughts reminded her. *As soon as I got you out of there.* He had thought of her too then, but she had let her fears swamp her and had run into the night. Had she really been fool enough to lose something that could have been so valuable because she'd been afraid she was like her mother?

Some cold, cruel little witch who stamped on his heart and then betrayed him without a care.

Esmeralda's words sounded over and over in her head, making her feel worse with every repetition. What if Nairo's sister had really not been mistaken? What if *she* was the one who had betrayed Nairo in this way?

What if he had once truly cared for her—all those years ago? And she had destroyed that caring by not trusting him so that now all he wanted was the blazing physical passion that had brought them together this time.

A passion that he had felt obliged to cover up by announcing their fake 'engagement' to the world. So that now he was tied into a relationship with her that he had never chosen or wanted.

'I can't do this,' she muttered, knowing from the sharp turn of his head, the dark, assessing glance down at her, that he had caught her words and knew exactly what she meant.

'You have to.'

'No, I don't—I can admit the truth, tell everyone that this engagement is a lie. Move out…'

At least that would free him. So why didn't he look pleased—relieved even?

'But that would break our contract.' His frown darkened dangerously. 'I can still take this commission from you, get someone else in to finish the dress.'

'You wouldn't!' Stark horror rang in Rose's voice. 'Not when Esmeralda's wedding is so close.'

'I would,' he returned, hard and sharp. 'If it meant stopping you from ruining her day by letting her know that what I've just told the press is a lie and so opening up a new sort of scandal that will have the paparazzi feasting on it like vultures for weeks.'

He would too, Rose realised. There was no doubt on that. He felt he had to make up to his sister for her losses—for what he saw as his abandonment of her when she needed him—and to do that he would pay any price. Even letting himself be bound into a fake relationship that he hated the idea of.

'I can't let you do that to her.'

And she couldn't do it either. She had grown so fond of Esmeralda over the past weeks, come to care for her.

'All right, then,' she agreed heavily.

It was only—what? Another couple of weeks and then she could…

Her mind flinched sharply away from the thought of what would happen then.

'Be assured you will still have the wedding commission and all that goes with it.'

He made it sound as if that were all that mattered, but then that was how he believed she felt. It was what she had set out to make him think she felt. The twist of pain in her gut had to be ignored if she was to go on. And she had to go on.

'OK,' she said slowly. 'I'll do it.'

'For Esmeralda?'

Of course, in his mind it could only be for Esmeralda. There was no one else who mattered.

'Of course for Esmeralda,' she said sharply. 'She and Oscar make a lovely couple and, like you, I'd hate it if anything prevented them from having their perfect day.'

Now what had she said that made his jaw clamp tight like that, the muscle at the side of his mouth clenching in uncontrolled response?

'Don't you believe me?' she asked uncomfortably.

For a long moment he looked down into her face.

Then, 'Oh, yes,' he said slowly. 'Yes, I believe you.'

It was the answer she wanted, but somehow it didn't give the reassurance she was looking for. There seemed to be so much behind the simple comment. With a brusque nod of agreement he turned and walked away down the hall, leaving her staring after him wondering why, when he'd said he believed her, he had left her feeling that he actually felt the exact opposite.

'And for you,' she suddenly found herself saying, the words escaping before she had time to think.

She would have caught them back if she could, but then she saw the way his long back stiffened as if a bullet had hit him between the shoulder blades and he came to an abrupt halt. Slowly he swivelled on his heels to turn round to face her.

'What?'

Too late to go back now, and, besides, she didn't want to withdraw the declaration even if he was glaring at her from beneath black brows drawn sharply together.

'Just what does that mean?'

'That I hope that when you've seen Esmeralda married to the man she loves, you'll finally feel that you've done your duty. That you'll have repaid whatever debt you feel you owed your sister—and even your father...'

'You think that's what all this is about?'

'I know it is.'

Though she had to admit that the deepening of that frown made that certainty falter badly.

'And I hope that maybe my part in all this will make up for the mistake I made in believing that you were involved in dealing drugs. I thought that was where you were getting the money you said would change our lives.'

'You didn't trust me enough to ask!'

There was something in his voice that tore into her heart and ripped it open. She deserved it, she knew, and she stiffened her spine to take the accusation that should have been made all those years ago.

'But I didn't trust you enough to tell you.' Nairo supplied the words she had hesitated to say.

'No, you didn't.' It was just a sigh. 'I thought I loved you, but I didn't know what loving someone really meant.'

She did now, and it was tearing her apart not to be able to say it. This time it was not a matter of trust, but knowing that this was not what he wanted from her. That the blazing heat of passion that they shared in bed was all that she meant to him.

'You can't really love where you don't really trust.'

'We were young—foolish—' Nairo's tone almost threw the words away. 'We had a lot of growing up to do.'

Rose could only nod mutely as she clamped her mouth shut on any thoughtless words she might let spill out and ruin the emotional truce they had reached. If this was the best she could have with Nairo, then she would take it.

'Now all we have to do is to see Esmeralda married,' Rose blurted out. Anything to remove that dark frown from between his eyes, lift the tension that held his jaw so tight. 'And then break off our fake engagement. That can't come soon enough.'

She couldn't keep him trapped longer than she was absolutely forced to.

'You promised...'

'I promised that no one would blame you for our break-up,' Nairo inserted, cold and steely. 'And you needn't worry—I'll keep that promise.'

'Good.' She even managed a smile to go with the word, though she prayed it didn't look as unconvincing as it felt. 'And then we can go our separate ways, knowing we owe each other nothing.'

Say no, she begged him in the privacy of her thoughts. *Tell me, just this once, that you don't want it to end this way.* If he even offered her an affair, for as long as it took to burn itself out between them, she would take that. She'd take anything if he'd just make her feel that she mattered to him, in this way at least.

Nairo's silence seemed to drag on and on, drawing out and out until she felt as if her already overstretched nerves might actually snap under the strain. But then at last he moved, nodding slowly.

'That would be the best way to handle this.'

'Then we'll keep to that business deal.'

Rose forced a smile onto stiff lips, though agreement was the last thing she felt. She even held out her hand as if she were still making the business deal he had first proposed to her. Her throat closed tight as Nairo took her fingers in his, her eyes blurring so that she missed the sudden change in his expression.

'No,' he shocked her by declaring sharply, his hand clenching around hers, holding tight as he whirled her towards him, right up against the warm, hard wall of his chest.

'There's more to it than that and you know it. There's this...'

His kiss plundered her mouth, crushing her lips back against her teeth, his tongue sliding along the space he had opened to him, tasting her, tormenting her.

'We've locked ourselves into this fake engagement now, the least we can do is to take advantage of it,' he muttered, rough and raw. 'I want you, and if you try to say that you don't want me, then I'll out you for the liar you are.'

'I— You...'

She tried to speak, but there was nothing to say. She'd told herself that if he had nothing to offer other than his passion, then that was what she would take for as long as it lasted. She wouldn't ask for anything more, knowing he had nothing to give.

So she gave up all attempts to think or to speak and sank into the warmth and strength of his embrace with a sound that was a sigh of acceptance and surrender and encouragement all in one.

'Yes,' she managed. 'Yes—I want you. I want this.'

For as long as it lasted.

CHAPTER TEN

'THAT LOOKS BEAUTIFUL...'

The voice in her ear made Rose start in surprise. With her head bent over the soft pink silk, her hands busy folding and pinning to get the perfect length for the skirt, she hadn't even been aware of the fact that Nairo had come into the room where she was working on the fitting for one of the bridesmaids' dresses. She didn't notice his arrival until he bent his head down to hers and pressed a kiss against her cheek.

Unable to look up at him, or find any words to respond, she simply nodded her head and focussed even more intently on the material in front of her, even though she knew that was not what was supposed to happen. Not when she was meant to be greeting her fiancé on his return after too long an absence away on business.

The feelings were there, it was just that she found it impossible to show them. He'd been away from the *castillo* for some days and she'd missed him more than she could imagine. It was a feeling that had been made all the worse by the knowledge that as the time drew closer to the actual date of Esmeralda's wedding, then so too the days of their 'engagement' must be counting down until the moment when the need for the pretence would be over and the break-up Nairo had promised he would choreograph would have to be set in motion.

When that happened she would have to pack her bags and leave. For good.

'Don't you agree, Marguerite?'

Nairo stunned her even more by turning nonchalantly away towards Oscar's stern matron of a mother, who had taken to supervising the preparations for the wedding, making sure that everything had her seal of approval before it was finalised, smiling easily.

'The dress is spectacular, isn't it? Your daughter will look wonderful in it.'

It was impossible not to contrast that easy question—and the duchess's equally relaxed agreement—with the way things had been just ten days ago. Before Nairo had announced their fake relationship to his family. After that, it had been as if the heating had been turned on in the house and the atmosphere had warmed steadily, even when Nairo wasn't there. Esmeralda, of course, had been overjoyed that her adored brother and her newfound friend had apparently fallen head over heels in love, and the Schlieburg family, even Duchess Marguerite, had thawed noticeably.

Not that this had made life any easier for Rose herself. Quite the opposite. The truth was that every moment was more uncomfortable, every glance, every smile, a torment when she knew they were all based on a lie, one she had to maintain because of her promise to Nairo. She was supposed to pretend that she was madly in love with him, a pretence that, deep inside, was frighteningly easy. Too easy, so that she felt she was in real danger of giving herself away to him while she knew that the softening of his voice when he spoke to her, the gentle touches on her arm or her waist and, worst of all, the softly lingering kisses that he drifted across her cheek or her lips, were just part of the act he had determined to play. One that he seemed better at playing, when there was nothing real in his feelings, than she was when her emotions were tearing her to pieces inside, making her feel as if she were bleeding to death from a thousand little cuts.

What made matters worse was the fact that she couldn't talk to anyone about their relationship.

Relationship! Hah! Rose let the pink silk drop from her hands as she lifted her finger to suck at the spot where a pin had gone in sharply and a tiny bead of blood had risen to the surface.

This was no *relationship*. The real truth was hidden away like a dark and dirty secret while every day she was treated with growing affection and welcomed into the family as if she really belonged there. But only for as long as Nairo would allow that to last.

'Careful! You don't want to mark it.'

He had seen the tiny damage she had inflicted on herself and he moved swiftly to ease the silk away so that there was no risk of her staining the beautiful material. But at the same time there was the touch of his other hand at the back of her neck, tracing over the knots of her spine where it was exposed by the way her head was bent over her work. The warmth of those strong fingers lingered, moving softly, stroking, circling over the bone at the nape of her neck, sending delicious shivers of response through her whole body.

'Come to me tonight,' he murmured against her ear, soft and low. 'Eleven o'clock…'

Another whisper meant for her alone and already Nairo was moving away, taking his caressing hand from her so that she felt a cold sense of loss that was a shadow over her heart. One that she couldn't help but contrast with Esmeralda's glowing happiness. Nairo's sister could bring her love for Oscar right out into the open for everyone to see, while Rose could only hide the truth of hers away. Holding it close to her heart while Nairo thought the way she was behaving was as much an act as his own performance.

It was a bitter irony that in those past days, when she had thought that she'd loved him, she had run away from revealing that love, not having the strength to hold on to it for better or worse. Now she knew how hard real love was to handle, she was strong enough—or did she mean weak enough?—to hold on as hard as she could until the day that this dream would come crashing down around her.

Perhaps it was that thought that made all the difference, or the days of his absence on a business trip were what made Nairo particularly passionate that night. She had barely arrived in the apartment before he snatched her up in his arms and carried her into the bedroom, dropping her down onto the bed with little ceremony. Then he proceeded to strip every item of clothing from her, giving her no time to feel the chill of the night air on her exposed flesh as he kissed and caressed his way down her, leaving her burning and tingling where his lips had touched.

By the time his hard body slid into her welcoming warmth she had been floating on a heated tide of hunger, yearning and open to him. The pulse that throbbed at her temples made her head swim so uncontrollably that she was thankful to be supported by the soft downy pillows. Her whole body felt as if it had dissolved into a pool of molten wax, lost, adrift, blind with her need for him.

That night her orgasm was so sharp, so overwhelmingly powerful that it seemed to split her mind in two, sending her spinning into the wildness of a world where nothing existed but herself, this powerful, passionate man and the exquisitely raw sensations they had created between them.

It took a long, long time for her to come back to reality. She had no idea how long she lay there, oblivious to everything but the man whose hard, warm chest cushioned her head, his ragged breathing slowly easing and his heart slowing from its frenzied race under her ear.

'That was special.' She couldn't hold it back even if it was the least she could tell him. 'So special.'

She felt the change in his mood in the way it affected the long, lean body lying beside her. From a sweat-sheened relaxation that came with intense sexual fulfilment, every muscle suddenly tightened, holding taut against her in a disturbing silence that pushed her to defiance.

'Oh, I know I would be a fool to think that you agreed with me.'

'It was special to me,' he said at last, his voice slow and dark. 'How could it not be? I've known the best sex I've ever had with you.'

If it was meant to be a compliment—and obviously that was the way that he intended she should take it—then it didn't have the desired effect. If sex was all it was, then it meant too little, nothing like the feelings she found herself longing for. Besides, it couldn't be true. No matter how she might long for even that little satisfaction.

'That's not really true,' she managed, unable to hold the words back.

'What?'

This time he pulled away from her, lifting himself up until he was propped against the carved wooden bedhead. Coldly searching eyes raked over her face.

'Just what the hell are you talking about?'

Could she, like him, tell the difference? Nairo wondered. The very thought rocked his sense of reality. *Noth-*

ing could ever match the way he had once felt about her. The searing burn of that long-ago innocence he had thought they had shared. From the first time, she had made everything make sense, made him want to change his direction in life, to change his world.

For her.

His head spun at the thought that she might even have sensed any feeling like that. Was there something in what he had done—the way he had kissed her, touched her, taken her body—that had risked exposing that hidden part of him to her? A part that not even his father, nor Esmeralda, had ever seen.

'Tell me,' he demanded. 'What the devil is that supposed to mean?'

She shifted in the bed beside him, lifting herself up till she was kneeling close, sitting back on her legs. She pulled the sheet with her, covering the pink-flushed delights of her body from him. It was that change in her mood, the need for concealment, that alerted him to the fact there was no room for dreams in what they had now. She still held her essential self apart from him, even when she had given him her body so willingly and openly.

'That there was someone very special once… No?' Rose questioned as she saw his head move in adamant denial.

'No one.'

'But Esmeralda said…'

The beautiful mouth that had just given her so much pleasure twisted sharply, giving her his response without him having to speak.

'My sister is a hopeless romantic. Besides, she was only a child at the time and she knew nothing. And now, all wrapped up in the fairy-tale details of her upcoming wedding, she still knows nothing of the truth of the basic facts of how it can be between a man and a woman.'

His tone formed the words into ice, making Rose shiver as they landed on her exposed skin, pulling the sheet closer round her for protection from their impact.

'And how is that?'

'Do you have to ask? You were there. You know what it was like.'

'Tell me,' she said, needing to know exactly what she was dealing with. 'How was it?'

That was almost a smile, she noted. But a smile that did nothing to warm the chills that had shuddered over her skin. Instead it made her shiver even more, deeply and inwardly.

'Couldn't be simpler,' Nairo stated. 'I had the hots for you and you had the hots for me.'

He reached out a hand, let his fingers trail across her shoulders and down to where the white sheet formed a tight but impossibly fragile barrier against his touch, his eyes darkening noticeably as they locked on to hers. She managed to control her response but only just.

'I still do—more so now you've grown up.'

Something in Nairo's face changed, sharpening that stare till it felt like the scrape of a blade across her skin.

'That was how it was for you too, wasn't it?'

Somewhere in the back of her mind, Rose acknowledged the death of the wild, foolish hope she had let half form.

'Oh, yes…'

Fearful that that probing gaze might discover more than was safe, she affected a tone of total nonchalance, even managing a sort of a smile, though it couldn't have been as careless as she had hoped for.

She'd prayed he'd forgive her for going to the police and that wish had been fulfilled. It was a long time ago he'd said, a third of a lifetime. So he'd shrugged off her foolishness, her naïveté in suspecting him. But behind that was the real, darker truth that he could shrug it off so easily, not because it hadn't mattered but because *she* hadn't mattered. Because he had never cared about her as she had cared about him.

'That was exactly how it was for me,' she managed even though the lie burned on her tongue like acid, threatening to make her stumble over the words.

Needing to protect herself from the way he made her feel, the way she was tempted to lay her soul open to him, she pushed herself out of the bed, wrapping the sheet round her and taking it with her.

'I'm starving,' she tossed over her shoulder at him, knowing she meant a very different form of hunger than the one that could be appeased with any amount of food. 'Want anything?'

'You know what I want,' he growled behind her, but to her surprise he snatched up his black towelling robe and followed her into the kitchen.

'So where did you go this time?' she asked a short while later, curled up on the settee and nibbling on the edge of some slices of apple, which were all that she could manage to prove her claim of hunger without them choking her.

'London. I had business there.'

Nairo fetched a glass of wine for them both, placing hers on the table before her while he lounged in one of the big dark red chairs, stretching his long legs out in front of him.

'Your mother's looking better,' he added unexpectedly.

'You went to see her?' Rose found it hard to believe, but he nodded easily.

'It seemed wrong to be so close and not check she was OK. And yes, she's doing fine. And she and Margaret are even better friends than before. She sends you her love.'

'Thank you! That means so much!'

It meant even more that he had put aside his own belief that she had forgiven her mother too easily in order to do this.

'I never thought...' she began, but Nairo was shaking his head, anticipating what she was about to say.

'I would never have been able to live with myself if I hadn't made peace with my father before he died,' he said, his voice rough and low. 'All I wanted was to be part of the family again. That's why I swallowed my pride...'

The way he tilted his glass, swallowed down some wine, revealed his feelings more than any words.

'Me too.' Rose dropped the apple slice down onto her plate, unable even to make a pretence at eating it. 'And I think I should say that's what Mum was looking for all her life—a sense of belonging.'

Something changed in Nairo's face, not exactly a softening, but his muscles lost some of their tension, the tautness of his jaw easing just a little.

'I brought you something.' He indicated with his glass, waving it in the direction of the dresser near the door. 'A gift.'

'You didn't need to...'

'Now what sort of a fiancé would I be if I didn't bring my betrothed a present to compensate for being away from her for so long? It's over there...'

Getting to her feet, the sheet wrapped round her trailing along in her wake, Rose moved as he directed.

'Here?' She let her fingers rest on the top of the briefcase he'd obviously deposited there as he arrived back home.

'Open it. It's not locked!' he added as she hesitated. 'Look inside.'

'I'm looking—' Rose stared into the open case. 'But what...?'

'In the bag—from the art gallery.'

He was watching intently as she picked up the cream paper bag with the name of a London art gallery on it in an elegant script. It was thin and flat as if there were nothing in it.

'This?' She frowned her confusion. 'But...'

There was just a single sheet of card inside the bag, a glossy postcard that shook in her grip as she tried to focus on it. It was an abstract design, glowing with colour. A splash of scarlet and gold and a deep clear turquoise that was her favourite colour ever.

'Lovely!' she managed, knowing there was something she was missing. 'It's gorgeous, but...'

When had he got up and come close to her? She hadn't seen him move and yet suddenly he was behind her, the heat of his body reaching her through the thin covering of the sheet.

'Turn it over.'

As he spoke he reached out to capture the fingers clasped on the edge of the card, lifting her hand to turn it over as he instructed, so that she could see the words written on the back: *Rosa in tramonta.*

'It means rose in sunset,' Nairo was explaining when she saw the rest of the inscription and knew exactly what he'd done. Why he'd done it. The room seemed to spin round her, everything blurring wildly.

'Enzo Cavalliero...' she managed through the tears that were streaming down her face. 'Enzo... My father...'

Twisting in his arms, she could only rest her damp face against his chest and weep out the tidal wave of emotions that had overwhelmed her.

'Hey...' His voice sounded odd, shaken. 'It was meant to please you.'

'And it does…' Rose drew in her breath on an unsteady hiccup. 'So much.'

'Bueno' was all he said. And then he just held her loosely, supporting her until the storm of emotion was over. At last, dashing a hand across her eyes and sniffing inelegantly, she regained some control and lifted her head to smile up into his watchful dark eyes.

'Thank you.' It was low and heartfelt. But she was surprised to see that no answering smile lit his face.

'I'm only sorry…'

Gently he lifted the card again, pointed to the dates. It took a moment, but then she realised what he was trying to tell her. Enzo Cavalliero had died very young.

Before she'd been born.

It took some long moments and a lot of hard swallowing before she could respond, nodding her head and managing at last to say in a whisper, 'No wonder my mother could never find him.' Her voice strengthened as she swallowed again. 'But at least she can know that he didn't abandon her…and me. Did you tell her?'

His rough shake of his head dismissed that idea.

'I thought you'd want to do that.'

He was so right about that. She couldn't wait to tell Joy, show her the postcard.

How different would her mother's life had been—and her own—if Enzo hadn't died so young? Perhaps she would never have run away from Nairo as she had if she'd had a family of her own, more reason to trust. But then there came the inevitable realisation that she would never have had to run from Fred Brown and so she'd never have met Nairo at all and that splintered her thought processes completely. All she could do was hold on to his hand, and the beautifully coloured card, and repeat sincerely, 'Thank you for this.'

It was when her mind and her eyes cleared as she turned back to close the briefcase that she stopped in astonishment as she saw what now lay on the top of it that had been hidden under the gallery bag at the start.

'What's— This is the house,' she said, picking up the photograph. 'The squat.'

It was no longer a squat. The large town house had been renovated, fully restored to its original elegance.

'What's this?' There was a large plaque at the side of the door. The words on it set her mind reeling again.

'Esmeralda House—a clinic…?'

'For anorexic girls,' Nairo supplied with obvious reluctance.

He didn't look at her but kept his gaze fixed on the photograph. Was he, like her, looking at that first-floor window as if it were possible that the ghosts of the people they had been ten years before might appear behind the glass?

'I didn't want the house for myself and I wanted to put it to good use. They can get medical and psychological help there. They can even live there under supervision until they get well.'

'What a wonderful idea!'

This time when she flung her arms round him it was with real delight and enthusiasm and she felt the stiffness of his long body hold for a moment, then slowly ease against her.

'I'm glad you think so.'

It was another moment before his hand came up to rest on her back, long fingers splayed out against her shoulder blades. The warmth of his touch set a whole new rush of sensations flooding through her. Not sexual but that sense of belonging that she had enjoyed since she had come to be part of the household here. The feeling of being part of a family in a way she'd never known before.

'Nairo,' she said quietly. 'Do you have a photo of her?'

She didn't explain who she meant and she knew she didn't have to. Already Nairo was reaching for his phone, scrolling through photographs until at last he held it out to her.

'That's Esmeralda?' She couldn't believe it—could barely recognise the bird-like creature she knew in the small, sturdy little girl with the huge dark eyes and the curling black hair. 'How old...?'

'Nine. Just before...'

Before he'd been driven out of the house by his lying stepmother, his angry father.

She knew what she wanted to say and suddenly, in this new atmosphere, she felt she could say it.

'Did that woman—Carmen—tell her she was fat?' She read the answer in the set of his face, the way that his jaw had clenched tight. 'How dare she?'

But he didn't want her to go any further, that much was obvious. So instead she took his hand and led him back to the big settee, pulling him down beside her, and leaning against him softly.

Taking his hand in hers, she stroked along his fingers, tracing the muscles, the veins.

'You can't blame yourself for Esmeralda's illness, you know.'

His hand jerked under hers, but she tightened her grip, holding him still.

'Your parents, your stepmother—they all did their part.'

'If I'd been here...'

'If your father had believed you, you would have been here.' Her voice rang with the confidence of knowing that was the truth. 'Nothing else would have stopped you.'

For a long, long moment he was silent and still, but when he spoke his lips were just against her temple.

'*Gracias,*' he said. '*Muchas gracias.*'

He didn't need to thank her, Rose thought. It was enough that he was here, holding her like this. She could stay here all night. But even as the thought crossed her mind she felt Nairo stir and he turned her hand so that now he was the one holding her fingers in his, the one stroking her hand.

Until he stopped dead, his touch and his focus resting on just one spot. At the bottom of the third finger of her left hand. Instantly she knew what was on his mind.

'No! I don't need a ring—I don't *want* a ring.' She prayed it sounded definite rather than desperate.

'Esmeralda asked about it. It's expected,' Nairo growled.

She couldn't bear it if he went any further. She already felt bad enough, fighting the urge to turn tail and run.

'It might be expected, it might be tradition, but this is a *lie!*'

Twisting in his hold, she came halfway across him, almost on his lap, as she set about distracting him the only way she knew how.

'An engagement ring should be about commitment,' she managed, pressing a kiss against his stubble-shadowed jaw and then moving up, one kiss at a time, towards his beautiful, sensual mouth, feeling the instant reaction in him and breathing a silent prayer of thanks for it. 'About togetherness—about love. But there's none of that here.'

Her hands stroked over his skin, caressing, teasing, awakening the need she wanted him to feel. His groan was a sound of surrender, one that told her she'd succeeded, even if deep down that was the last thing she wanted. She welcomed the hunger and demand of his response in the same moment that it tore her heart in two.

With only the slightest tug he released the derisory protection of the fine cotton sheet, letting it fall to the side, exposing her nakedness to him once more.

Nairo's hand smoothed over her skin, along the curve of her hip and sliding upwards over her ribcage to curl around and cup the heaviness of one breast. He let one finger trail over the darker-toned nipple and watched as if hypnotised the way that the skin puckered and pouted under his touch. His smile was a slow, lazy curl of his lips before he bent his head and let his tongue circle the raised bud. The warm breath of his laughter made her draw in her own air on a gasp of delight before he took the sensitised skin into the heat and moisture of his mouth, tugging on it softly in a way that sent the burn of desire flashing along every nerve in her body.

'I've never known love,' he murmured against her, making her quiver and squirm against the softness of the white linen sheet. 'Never wanted it, but, *infierno*, *querida*, when things are this damn good, then who needs love?'

'No…one,' Rose managed on a gasp. 'No one could want anything more.'

Even the deep-down knowledge that she was lying, that she desperately longed for so much more, couldn't enforce the restraint she knew she should impose on herself. Restraint had nothing to do with this—it was all sensuality. The glorious wild storm of passion that was swamping her, driving away every other thought from her mind.

She wanted so much more than this. Needed more from this man than the feelings he had brusquely described as 'the hots'. She wanted things that were a lifetime, an eternity, away from what he was prepared to give her. But she wanted *him* so much that she couldn't bear to drag herself away and turn her back on the little he did have to offer her.

So she let him pull her down beside him, felt the rest of the sheet torn away and tossed aside, her pulse thundering rough and raw as he moved to come over her, the heat and hardness of his body searing over hers. His mouth took hers, his hair-roughened legs coming between hers, nudging them aside to let the blunt heat of his erection push at the moist core of her being that so longed for him.

She was open to him already. Lost to herself, given up entirely to him and oblivious of anything else. She was all sensation, all heat. All longing, all need. And that was all that mattered right now.

'Oh, yes,' she told herself, whispered against his ear as she pulled him closer, adjusted her body so that he could feel the need she had for him. 'Yes!'

Tomorrow would come soon enough and she would have to face what tomorrow would bring. But for here and now, for tonight—if only for tonight—as Nairo had said, when things were this damn good, then who needed love?

If she said it often enough, then she might just come to believe it.

CHAPTER ELEVEN

'I'VE HAD A wonderful time, Rosalita! Everyone said how absolutely beautiful my dress was.'

Esmeralda accompanied her joyful words with an enthusiastic hug, squeezing all the breath out of Rose and taking away her ability to answer at the same time.

'Just think—next time it will be your big day!'

But that was a step too far. With its scenes of joy and promise, the declarations of love and commitment, it had been inevitable that Esmeralda's wedding day would be an ordeal, but two things had combined to make it even worse than she had anticipated.

The fake engagement was bad enough and she had struggled to accept the congratulations of so many of the guests at today's event. Her head had pounded, her jaw muscles had ached from the effort of forcing a fake smile onto her lips. But the last twist of the knife had arrived in the shape of a letter that had been delivered to her room only that morning. She had discovered it lying on her dressing table when she had crept back into the house from Nairo's apartment, just in time to help Esmeralda prepare for her wedding, and the memory of its contents had haunted her all through the day.

She couldn't meet Esmeralda's wide brown eyes, knowing the questioning look that would be in them. So she stared fixedly over to the side of the room to avoid it. But that only made matters so much worse when she spotted the tall, darkly elegant figure of Nairo making his way towards them.

Knowing that he believed she couldn't lie to save her life, she had hoped that she would be able to keep away from him today, at least until she got some control over her face and her thoughts. But she had forgotten that Esmeralda had wanted her to be waiting at the door of the cathedral, ready to make any last-minute adjustments to the dress before she began her walk up the aisle.

'I can't wait for you to become my sister!' she had said.

Rose had hated having to lie to Esmeralda and the knowledge that very soon she would have to disillusion the girl who had become such a close friend to her was more than she could bear. Now that Esmeralda was happily married, and Nairo had achieved his stated aim, then surely the end couldn't be long in coming, and the report in the newspaper cutting that had been in that envelope, with the photograph that brought such bittersweet memories along with it, must surely mean that she was already living on borrowed time.

'We don't want to rush into anything,' she managed painfully, aware of the fact that Nairo was prowling nearer.

'Don't want to rush!' Esmeralda laughed up into her brother's watchful face. 'Oh, come on, Nairo—what do you call rushing? I mean, you haven't even given dear Rose a ring.'

This time Rose couldn't hold her feelings in check as her gaze flew to Nairo's face, clashing with the hard stare of his bronze eyes with a sensation like slamming into a brick wall. Were his thoughts too filled with the memories of the night she'd told him she couldn't bear to wear such a symbol of the lie they were living?

'I don't need a ring,' she put in hastily. 'Really I don't…'

But Esmeralda was not to be diverted. 'I don't understand you, *hermano*…' She shook her head at her brother. 'Now that you've finally found someone you can love, wouldn't you want to let the world know about it? I know I would!'

'But you, little sister, just want everyone to share in all the fripperies and the fancies that make up your idea of a romantic wedding.'

As always when he spoke to his sister, Nairo's tone was warm and indulgent, making Rose struggle against the bitterness of knowing that she would only ever share in that warmth as an act put on to present a false image of their relationship.

Desperately she lifted the beautiful crystal glass she was holding to her lips, hoping that a swallow of champagne would at least ease the painful dryness in her throat. She felt as if she had been struggling to breathe through the tightness in her heart since the moment she had watched Nairo take his sister's arm in order to lead her down the aisle to her groom.

This might be his sister's wedding, but that image of Nairo, sleekly elegant in the fitted formal wear, was the way that he would look at his own marriage, with the slender figure of a bride at his side in a dress of beautiful white lace, with a delicate veil cascading down from her head. She had no idea who that future bride might be. She only knew that it would never be her.

'But I came to tell you that your new husband is looking for you—and I need to claim my fiancée. Rose and I need to talk.'

He hadn't needed to add the second half of his comment; the mention of Oscar had been more than enough to have Esmeralda turning and setting off in his direction before Nairo had even finished speaking. Leaving Rose alone with the man whose looming presence sent uncomfortable shivers of nerves skittering up and down her spine.

'Talk about what?' she asked sharply, knowing immediately it was the wrong thing to say and the wrong way to say it.

'Not here,' he responded, his voice as flat and expressionless as his face. 'Come with me.'

His grip on her hand was hard and tight, and he set off in the opposite direction to his sister without looking back to see if Rose was following him. Of course she was; it was either that or be dragged along in his wake.

How many difficult and life-changing conversations had begun with the words *we need to talk*? Rose asked herself as she stumbled after Nairo. Once out in the hall, with the doors closed behind them, the buzz of conversation died away to just a low hum and the house seemed suddenly cold and silent, alien somehow. Only now did Rose realise how much she had come to love living at the *castillo*. Not because of its size and luxuriousness but because over the past weeks it had felt like home to her too, she realised, living there in security and peace for perhaps the first time in her life. The nights she had spent with Nairo had been the glorious icing on the cake that was the sense of coming home, so much so that she had pushed away to the back of her mind the realisation of the fact that before too long, she would no longer belong here.

But wasn't the truth that she had never actually *belonged* here?

The time with Nairo was ticking away too, and she'd known this moment had to come. She just hadn't expected it to come quite this fast. The ink was barely dry on Esmeralda's wedding certificate, but it seemed her brother was already looking for his freedom. Well, she wasn't going to beg for more time. She'd gone into this with her eyes open, and if this was what had to be, then she'd face it with as much dignity as possible.

Don't worry—I'll take the blame... All you'll have to do is to look like the broken-hearted fiancée.

There would be no hardship there. When she left here she wouldn't need to pretend that her heart was shattered. She would leave it behind her, in Nairo's keeping, and would have to try to find a way to live without it.

'In here...'

The library was as far as possible away from the ball-room, and it had a door that locked. Perhaps that would guarantee them the privacy he needed, Nairo told himself as he led her into the room he'd decided was the best place for this. If there was such a thing as a 'best place' for this. Just as there was never going to be a 'best time' for it either.

The truth was that this was probably going to be the worst possible time to have this confrontation with Rose. But he had been living a lie for too long now and he couldn't let the situation continue a moment longer.

Today had been the last straw. He had had to watch Esmeralda light up like a brilliant star, her joy blazing in her eyes. He had felt the tremors of emotion run through the fingers that rested on his arm as he walked her down the aisle. Tremors that had vanished in an instant as she had seen Oscar turn to face her, his own smile mirroring hers.

It had been that smile that had shaken him out of the reverie he had slipped into. Just for a moment, wildly, crazily, dangerously, he had actually found himself imagining that *he* had been the one heading for the altar—with Rose as his bride...

Coming back to reality had been like being slapped hard

in the face, and it had forced him to acknowledge there was no way he could let this situation continue as it was.

He was in danger of finding himself back in the same sort of mess as he'd faced ten years before if he wasn't careful. Had he really learned so little in the intervening time? That was when he had known that he had to speak to Rose, and as soon as possible.

But now that he was here, in this quiet room, turning the key in the door against intruders, it seemed that all words had deserted him.

'Is this going to be so bad that you have to lock me in?'

Rose's voice was high and rather tremulous, though she flashed a smile that was clearly meant to make him think she had used the line as a joke.

'I'm keeping others out, rather than locking us in.'

Though he didn't think she'd stay around long once he'd told her what he had to say. She'd been reluctant to come here from the start and now it seemed that she was positively itching to get away.

When all he wanted to do was to keep her with him.

He'd known he was in trouble in the moment that she had moved forward to help Esmeralda arrange her dress when they had stepped out of the limousine onto the stone steps of the cathedral. Everyone who had seen his sister in her wedding finery had exclaimed in delight at the vision she presented. But for Nairo there was only one woman in the whole of Spain in that moment.

Her dress was an old gold colour, silky and close-fitting, with touches of lace at the shoulders and hem. Her auburn hair had been gathered up under a ridiculous frivolity of a hat, nothing more than a couple of feathers in a colour that exactly matched that dress, and just the way those feathers nodded and danced in the breeze made his heart clench on a clutch of need. He had rarely seen her wearing much make-up at any time, but today the subtle use of shadow made her hazel eyes seem huge and dark, and her lips looked full and soft, touched with a shimmer of colour. How he had stopped himself from giving in to the hunger that burned through him, tilting up that determined little chin and planting a hard, demanding kiss on that luscious mouth, he would never know. He'd had an ugly fight with his most primitive needs right there in the porch of the cathedral and he was having exactly the same battle right now.

Especially when she reached up and unpinned the perky little hat, tossing it onto a nearby table and shaking back her hair in a gesture that spoke of relief and freedom. One that almost broke his resolve to hold on to his control.

'I know what this is all about,' she said, her voice sounding as uneven and jerky as the pulse that was battering at his temples.

'You do?'

He had thought he had managed to hide his true feelings throughout the day.

But then he realised that she had opened the small boxy clutch bag she carried and was pulling something out of it. A creased piece of newspaper.

She unfolded the paper, slapped it down on the table in front of him. But he didn't need to see it. He knew exactly what she was trying to show him. It was the same photograph that had hit him right between the eyes when he had opened the paper that morning.

'Ah...' he said flatly. 'That.'

'Yes—that.'

Narrow fingers tipped with soft rose-pink polish reached for the paper again, and, intriguingly, he noticed that they shook a little as they did so.

She touched the photograph briefly, then looked up at

him, green-brown eyes dark like the water in the depths of a bottomless, shadowed pool.

'That was what you wanted to *talk about*, wasn't it?'

The emphasis on the two words made him wince inwardly. She was sounding altogether more challenging than he had expected. Had he got this all wrong?

'Partly.'

He wasn't giving anything away, Rose reflected. The single-syllable answers told her nothing, and surprisingly she couldn't see the anger she'd expected in his face. Or was he just better at hiding it than she'd imagined?

She flattened the newspaper again, so that the face in the picture stared up at her from the photograph.

Her own face.

It was a tiny, tatty old passport-style photograph. The sort that was taken in a photograph booth, four prints for a few pounds. It showed every day of its ten years of age, and she knew that age to the exact day. It was one copy of the photograph that she and Nairo had taken in a rare moment of indulgence. Nairo was laughing into the camera while she had her lips pressed tight against his cheek in a playful kiss.

The photo had been published in the UK papers as well as the Spanish ones and the headline in the copy she had read: 'Hola de Nuevo! *Long-Lost Lovers Reunited.*'

The story below it told how 'billionaire Spanish entrepreneur Nairo Moreno knew his beautiful fiancée, designer Rose Cavalliero, many years ago'. The whole story of their life in the squat had been dragged up again, even with a photograph of the once near-derelict building as it was now repaired and restored to its former glory. But no mention of the use to which it was now being put.

The story of the drugs raid had been excavated too, the report of the police investigation repeated over again. Only right at the bottom did it say that Nairo had been found completely innocent.

She knew what seeing this report must have done to Nairo, the anger he must have felt. Surely he would believe there could only be one person who had provided the information to the press. All day she'd been expecting the volcano to explode at any moment; she was just stunned to find that his anger was such an icy, controlled response rather than the eruption she'd been expecting.

'Tell me about it,' Nairo said, and there was a subtle change in his voice. No anger. No recrimination. Instead she might almost have said that he sounded as if he had lost something very important. It was strange because that was the exact way she was feeling too.

Swallowing hard, she had to draw on all the courage she could find inside. She'd sold him short ten years before by not talking to him openly; she wasn't going to do it this time.

'The photo—' she began, her mouth so dry that she found it hard to form the words. 'I didn't...'

'No—you didn't. But I kind of wish you had.'

'You—what...?'

Coherent thought deserted her. She could only stand and stare into the clouded golden eyes that had turned opaque and hidden.

'You didn't give the photo, the report, to the papers. I know you didn't. You couldn't. You would never hurt someone you love that way.'

A rush of relief was blended with another very different strain of emotion. How did he know? How had he guessed? What had she done to give herself away? And how was she supposed to cope with the fact that he'd guessed and yet he looked so uninvolved—so *disappointed*?

'You would never do that to Esmeralda on her wedding day.'

Now her head was really spinning. She had come in here expecting the outbreak of war, to be told to pack her bags and get out, but instead she was confronted by this deadly quiet man with the almost colourless face, the deep dark eyes, and suddenly she didn't know who Nairo was or what he wanted from her.

'I don't understand.'

Her legs felt weak as cotton wool so that suddenly she plumped down into the nearest chair, grabbing hold of the arms for support. But that just made things so much worse. Nairo's dark figure towered over her, making her feel very small and vulnerable.

'What has Esmeralda to do with this?'

That made his face change at least, but the way it brought the frown back to between his dark brows didn't help at all.

'Surely it's obvious. I've seen you with Esmeralda. I know that you care for her. You wouldn't do this to her.'

She wanted to smile, she wanted to laugh, she wanted to break down and bury her head in the cushions on the chair, weeping her heart out. She wanted to do all three at once. Shockingly, it was laughter that won and she heard the strangled, slightly hysterical sound echo round the elegant room.

'You know I didn't do this—for Esmeralda?'

His frown this time was one of genuine confusion.

'Of course—who else?'

'Oh, Nairo, don't you know?'

As soon as she asked the question the stab of a shard of ice right in her heart gave her her answer. Of course he didn't know. He could see the way she felt about his sister, but to the way she felt about him he was totally blind.

Either because he just couldn't see, or because he didn't *want* to.

It was then that something hit her like a light bulb going on inside her head. Of course! She was the one who couldn't see. He had promised to give her a reason to break off their engagement. One that everyone would understand, and this…

'Look. I know you want this over and done with!'

She pushed herself to her feet again, unable to hold back, not caring if she let him into the way she was really feeling. It was too late to worry about that.

'But really, don't you think you could have waited—that you could have had a bit more consideration? Today was supposed to be Esmeralda's perfect day. She's so happy… What do you think she'll feel when she realises that our engagement has broken up—today of all days?'

'It has to be today,' Nairo flung at her, his voice raw with emphasis. 'There's no other way. Because I can't live like this. I can't live this lie any longer.'

CHAPTER TWELVE

SHE COULDN'T KNOW what it had done to him to lie all this time, Nairo admitted inwardly. To fake the feelings or, rather, to show the feelings and know that she believed they were faked, put on for show to convince everyone else and meaning nothing.

What was that saying 'fake it till you make it'? Hadn't the last weeks been such hell because he had been *making* it for so many days now while all the time the person he most wanted to persuade was convinced that he was doing the perfect job of faking it as they'd agreed? That was what he couldn't bear to live with any longer.

The truth was that he'd hoped for something else, he admitted bitterly. He'd hoped that when he let Rose know that he trusted her, totally sure that she hadn't been the person who had sent the photograph and the story to the press, then things would change. He strongly suspected he knew who had done that and it wasn't her. It had all the hallmarks of Jason's nasty-minded tricks and schemes to make a profit out of someone else's upset. Though how he'd got hold of the photo in the squat he had no idea.

But the real culprit didn't matter. What mattered was the fact that he believed in Rose. For perhaps the first time in his life he had put all his trust in a person—a woman—who wasn't part of his family. He had brought her here to demonstrate that trust and deep down he'd hoped that when he'd done so she might rethink the idea of breaking off this false engagement, going their separate ways.

That had failed miserably. Bitter laughter caught in his throat, making him cough, and he was grateful for the way that needing to cover his mouth with his hand gave him a chance to hide what he was feeling, to hold back the words that he came so dangerously close to letting slip. The ones she clearly didn't want to hear.

'No more lies!' he managed, forcing the words out so that they sounded as cold and as brutal as her *I know you want this over and done with!* Anything else would have stuck in his throat.

No more lies. Rose had to struggle to catch the words because they seemed to get tangled up in the cough that shook Nairo's throat—or was it a laugh? She couldn't see what there was to laugh about.

But then she remembered how just a few minutes before, she had let go and laughed herself, when laughing was the last thing she felt like doing. When she really wanted to just break down and weep.

Thinking back, she knew he had said something…but she couldn't make it make any sense.

She didn't give the photograph to the press, she had said, and he had replied…

'No—you didn't. But I kind of wish you had.'

She only realised that she had repeated the words out loud when she saw him nodding along with them, a strange little smile curling at the corners of his mouth as he raked both his hands through the darkness of his hair, ruffling it impossibly.

'I'm a fool, aren't I?' he stunned her by responding. 'A blind, crazy fool. But I did hope.'

The tousled effect of his hair falling softly over his forehead gave him an impossibly young and boyish look that tugged on something vulnerable in her heart. She hardly dared to ask, but she had to take the risk because if she missed this chance it might be the only one she would ever get.

'Why would you…?' Her voice shook with disbelief. 'How could you ever *hope* that I'd sent the photo to the papers?'

Nairo sank back against the huge polished oak table in the middle of the room, staring down at his feet, shaking his head as if in disbelief at his own behaviour.

'So that then I'd know you kept the photo.'

'Do you *still* want proof?'

Had she been a fool to let herself hope? She couldn't believe how close she had come to letting him in and now it seemed that she had been blindly led along by what she most wanted rather than what he had actually meant.

'Rose—no…'

His movement towards her was rough, almost desperate, his hand coming out to her. But she was already reaching into her purse, yanking out the small photograph and tossing it down onto the table. That would show him she hadn't parted with her copy of the picture to any reporter.

'I don't need any proof at all. I know exactly what you mean.'

'You do?'

It was meant to sound unconvinced, totally sceptical. But there was something in his tone and in his face that shook the conviction she needed so that instead her words were only questioning, suddenly uncertain.

'I do. Because of this…'

Nairo's hand slid into his pocket, pulled out a black leather wallet and opened it. The small piece of paper he took out and placed on the table beside the one she'd

just tossed down had a black-and-white image on it just
the same.

Except that on this one it was Rose who was looking
straight into the camera, her mouth stretched wide in a
smile. And Nairo was the one who had his lips pressed
against her cheek.

'You…' It was all that Rose could manage, the sight of
the two photographs side by side taking any other words
away.

It was the fact that he waited, silent and still, that got to
her in the end. It gave her a strange sort of hope, one that
she would never have found in any words he might say.

'You kept the photograph—but why?'

'Because I never wanted to forget you.'

Forget her or forget what she'd done? The way she'd
treated him.

'When I saw the photo in the paper I hoped that was
what it meant to you too. That you had kept your copy,
perhaps for the same reason.'

Shockingly, Rose saw that the fingers that reached for
her copy of the photograph were not quite steady.

'But I knew you would never have done that. You just
couldn't.'

The revelation of his total trust was so huge, so important, that it rocked her mind and for a moment she had
to turn off onto a mental siding, another topic, while she
gathered her thoughts.

'Who do you think did that?'

'Who gave it to the press?' Nairo asked. 'Jason, I expect. That night he vowed he'd have his revenge on you—
on both of us. He must have decided this was worth a try
to come between us.'

'Come between us,' Rose echoed. 'But was there ever
an "us" to divide?'

'Can you doubt it? Look at those pictures—'

A long forefinger dropped onto the one he had pulled from his wallet. The one where he was kissing her cheek, his eyes closed in an expression of absolute happiness.

'The day we took those felt like a whole new beginning for me. That was the day I first contacted my father, told him I was prepared to apologise.'

That rocked Rose's sense of reality.

'But you'd done nothing wrong—why apologise?'

'If that was what it took. I wanted to turn my life around—make a fresh start. I wanted to have more to offer you than a dreadful room in a scruffy squat. I wanted to take you to Spain—bring you here. Give you a home—with me.'

'Instead I messed it all up for you.'

And for herself. She'd lost her chance to make that new start in life with Nairo. The pictures of the two of them blurred through the film of bitter tears.

'It was my fault as much as—more than—yours,' Nairo said urgently. 'I didn't trust you enough to tell you. Didn't trust you with my real name or my hopes to reunite with my family. I was never honest with you about my feelings. I haven't been even now.'

'Even now?' What did she take from that? Rose had no idea at all and she was afraid to hope.

'When I saw how the paparazzi were hounding you, I thought it would be too much for you. You wouldn't be able to take the press attention all over again and you'd leave.'

'You came to my rescue.'

'No.' It was hard, forceful. 'I couldn't let you go, but I was a coward and didn't tell you why. So I pushed you into an engagement, hung it on the importance of Esmeralda's big day. I had to keep you here until we had a chance to try again. But why would you want to try again if I was never honest with you about my feelings?'

'And what are those feelings?'

It was the question she had to ask, but he would never know how much courage it took her to make it. A direct question demanded a direct answer, but what if the response was not the one she longed for?

Nairo drew in a long, ragged breath, reached out to touch the photographs again as if they were some sort of talisman.

'I wanted to get the wedding out of the way so that then maybe we could have our own time.'

Our own time sounded wonderful, but what she needed was a future. She'd tried to tell herself that she would accept what they had for as long as he let her, but watching Esmeralda today she had known that just wasn't enough. It was all or nothing. She couldn't accept anything else.

'Nairo—we agreed.'

'I know we agreed.' It was dark, raw, vehement. 'And I'll keep to that if I have to. If you still want me to give you an excuse to break us apart and let everyone know this engagement is over, then I promised and I'll keep that promise. But don't ask me to make it look as if I want someone else—as if I love someone else. I can't do that. I once told you that you couldn't lie to save your life and on this neither can I. It would be a lie to make it look as if I care for anyone else. Even for you.'

This time his shake of the head was more violent, sending his already impossibly tumbled hair flying until it fell back in even more disarray than before.

'I can't lie like that even to give the one person I really love her freedom.'

The one person I really love. Rose's heart was thundering, her pulse racing. Had she heard right? Had he really said…?

'In fact I can't let you go at all.'

Again he pushed both hands through the now wildly ruffled black hair, the gesture expressing so much more than his carefully controlled words.

'I know you stayed for Esmeralda…'

'It wasn't just for Esmeralda. How could it be when I—'

'You love her,' he inserted, and the odd shake in his voice did more to convince her than anything else he had done or said.

'I love her—for herself of course,' Rose told him softly. 'But perhaps even more than that I love her because she's a part of the family of someone who means the world to me. Because she loves and is loved by someone I love more than life.'

'Who?'

It rasped from a throat that sounded constricted as if he was having to fight to get it out. But there was no fight left in his eyes. Their bronze depths were clear and unshadowed, totally open to her, hiding nothing of the way he was feeling. That feeling gave her heart such a lift that she felt almost as if her feet had left the floor as she smiled at him, straight into those eyes, everything she dreamed of sharing showing in her own face.

'Oh, Nairo—do you have to ask? I love you with all my heart.'

She needed to make the first move now, stepping forward, reaching out to him. But he met her more than halfway, gathering her up into his arms and crushing her against him as his mouth came down hard on hers.

It was all that Rose had ever dreamed of. All she had hoped for but never believed it would come true. She was here, in Nairo's arms, and to him she was *the one person I really love*. She couldn't ask for anything more.

But Nairo, it seemed, had one more thing he needed to say. Slowly, softly, reluctantly he released her, searching in his jacket pocket for something. The leather box he pulled out was obviously old, worn, slightly battered.

'Esmeralda said I'd never given you a ring. I know how you feel about that—but this is different.'

'How *I felt*,' Rose inserted gently, needing to put every last misunderstanding behind them.

He looked down at the box in his hand, closed his fingers around it, then opened them again.

'I brought this with me because I wanted to ask you to marry me properly. To do me the greatest honour of being my wife—but now...'

He frowned, tightened his hold on the box again and shook his head.

'This is the ring I'm supposed to offer. It's tradition—the family ring—one handed down from generation to generation and so it's the ring I'd want you to have. But my father gave it to my mother—and look how that worked out. I didn't think you'd want something that came with that shadow over its history.'

'Oh, Nairo...'

The fact that he cared, that he'd even stopped to consider that, told her more about his feelings than any more flowery declarations of love and devotion. He wanted her to have his family ring—but he wanted it to be right for her. He didn't want them to end up at war, separated like his parents, who had scarred the family so badly.

'But there were others who wore it, weren't there?' she said softly.

He nodded slowly, dark eyes locked with hers.

'My grandfather gave it to my grandmother and he and

Abuela were married for almost sixty years. And their parents before them.'

Rose couldn't hold back her smile. He needed that and she wanted to give it to him.

'So its history is not all bad, my love. There was just that one blip—and we can break away from that. We can make it a ring of love and happiness all over again.'

It was as if a light had been switched on behind his eyes. His head came up, his long body straightening as if a huge weight had been lifted from his shoulders. His own lips curved into an echoing smile as he flipped open the box, displaying the magnificent diamond ring it enclosed.

'We can—and we will, *mi amor*,' he declared in a voice that resonated with confidence and, more importantly, with a newfound happiness. 'I could ask for nothing more than to spend the rest of my life making you, my beautiful wife, the happiest woman in the world, if you'll let me.'

'Oh, yes—yes, please!' was all that Rose could manage before he caught her to him again and crushed her lips in a kiss that sealed his promise for the rest of their days together.

* * * * *

If you enjoyed this story, check out these
other great reads from Kate Walker:
DESTINED FOR THE DESERT KING
OLIVERO'S OUTRAGEOUS PROPOSAL
A QUESTION OF HONOUR
A THRONE FOR THE TAKING
THE DEVIL AND MISS JONES
Available now!

MILLS & BOON®

MODERN™

POWER, PASSION AND IRRESISTIBLE TEMPTATION

MILLS & BOON®

EXCLUSIVE EXCERPT

Dante Di Sione can't believe the beautiful blonde
who 'accidentally' stole his family's tiara is black-
mailing him – for a date to her sister's wedding!
If Willow wants to be his fake fiancée, she'll
have to play the part to the full. Only Willow's
confidence is fake…and she's a virgin!

Read on for a sneak preview of
DI SIONE'S VIRGIN MISTRESS
the fifth in the unmissable new eight book Modern series
THE BILLIONAIRE'S LEGACY

"I'm sorry. I'm out of here."

"Dante…"

"No. Listen to me, Willow." There was a pause while
he seemed to be composing himself, and when he
started speaking, his words sounded very controlled.
"For what it's worth, I think you're lovely. Very lovely.
A beautiful butterfly of a woman. But I'm not going
to have sex with you."

She swallowed. "Because you don't want me?"

His voice grew rough. "You know damned well I
want you."

She lifted her eyes to his. "Then why?"

He seemed to hesitate and Willow got the distinct
feeling that he was going to say something dismissive,
or tell her that he didn't owe her any kind of explanation.

But to her surprise, he didn't. His expression took on that almost gentle look again and she found herself wanting to hurl something at him…preferably herself. To tell him not to wrap her up in cotton wool the way everyone else did. To treat her like she was made of flesh and blood instead of something fragile and breakable. To make her feel like that passionate woman he'd brought to life in his arms.

"Because I'm the kind of man who brings women pain, and you've probably had enough of that in your life. Don't make yourself the willing recipient of any more." He met the question in her eyes. "I'm incapable of giving women what they want and I'm not talking about sex. I don't do emotion, or love, or commitment, because I don't really know how those things work. When people tell me that I'm cold and unfeeling, I don't get offended—because I know it's true. There's nothing deep about me, Willow—and there never will be."

Don't miss
DI SIONE'S VIRGIN MISTRESS
by Sharon Kendrick

Available November 2016